Supernatural

Featuring stories by:
J.A. Cummings
Nichole Craig
Alanna Robertson-Webb
Jennifer Carr
Liam Pritchard
Patrick Tibbits
C. Marry Hultman
Kimberly Gray
Katelyn Cameron
Monica Shultz
Shashi Kadapa

Published by Irish Horse Productions, 2020

Supernatural

© 2020 Irish Horse Productions

All rights reserved. No part of this book may be reproduced or transmitted in any form or by any electronic or mechanical means, including photocopying, recording, or by any information storage and retrieval system, without permission in writing from the publisher, except by reviewers, who may quote brief passages in a review.

This is a work of fiction. Names, places, characters, and events are the product of the author's imagination. Any resemblance to any persons, living or dead, is entirely coincidental.

This book is to be sold to ADULT AUDIENCES ONLY. It contains adult content which may be offensive to some readers.

Cover Art © 2020 CJ Graphics & Design
Published by Irish Horse Productions
Edited by Sassa Brown

Warning: The unauthorized reproduction or distribution of this copyrighted work is illegal. Criminal copyright infringement, including infringement without monetary gain, is investigated by the FBI and is punishable by up to 5 years in prison and a fine of $250,000.

Table of Contents

The Guns of Autumn 6
The Farm in the Forest 36
Elle 51
Home to Heaven 65
Guardian Lycan 70
Lia's Tale The Secret of the Rowan ... 79
The Day the River Freezes 91
Silent Moments 101
I Could Not Stop for Death 110
The Other War 129
And the Windows Shook 153
Postman from the Other Side 188

The Guns of Autumn
By J.A. Cummings

During the dark days of the Great War, a French field nurse risks everything to rescue the man she loves with the help of a very unusual guide.

France
October 1915

Brown and yellow fallen leaves skittered across the marble floor like frightened mice, blown by the wind that entered the church the same way she had. The hole in the wall, caused by one of a hundred thousand falling bombs, had given Christine Rheault the access she needed to enter the church. The door was impassable, blocked by the fallen timbers of what once had been the spire, and with the rubble of the blasted tower strewn across the entrance, there was no way she could have used the narthex.

She slipped along what remained of the wall, headed toward the transept and the altar where the crucifix still hung, sorrowing over the sinful nature of mankind and the new glut of b blood sacrifices that had been slain for the sin of pride. Given the things that she had seen on in the field hospitals where she worked, Christine believed that Jesus would be weeping for the rest of time.

She knew that she would be.

This had been her village church in the happy times before the war had come. She had been baptized here, using holy water from the now-demolished font. She had hoped that one day she would be married here, as well. That was never going to happen now.

Richard Belvoir had been her first love, beginning when they were just children in school.

He was the first boy to ever give her a rose, the first to declare his love, the first to kiss her lips. There was another first that she had hoped for, but time and the machinations of men and kings had interfered. Now it was likely that he would never be her first lover because word had reached their village that Richard was wounded and left for dead on the field when his fellow soldiers had retreated from the battle. The guns were too persistent that autumn, they said, to allow anyone to go out looking for him, and so they left him in the shell hole where he'd taken refuge.

Christine worked as a nurse, a secular adjutant to the Sisters of Mercy, the nuns who had run her Catholic secondary school. The nuns had left as a group to serve the needs of the wounded and dying when the war began. She had been in field hospitals when the trains of wounded had come streaming in from the bloodbaths that generals called battles. Men with missing limbs, men with shattered faces, men with hanging... *enough*. She closed her eyes hard against the images that rose in her mind, images that threatened to overwhelm her at random hours of the day. She would not think of these things now, especially not when every man she saw in her mind's eye now wore Richard's face.

Autumn was normally a magical time in this part of France. The trees stood blazing in the light of a sun that was still bright and warm, the forests giving up the last of their leaves in a display of glory that could never be matched. In any other year, there would be harvest festivals, and the bottling of that year's wine and the golden wheat would be brought in from the fields in groaning wagons. Autumn was a joyous time.

Not this year.

This year, there was no wheat. The fields around Mondraux had been churned into mud and shell holes, and the only crop they brought in now was dead and dying men. The people of her village would go hungry this winter since they had been unable to salvage enough grain to feed themselves through the lean months ahead. War was hell not only for the men who fought. It was hell to try to just keep living when the war was fought where you had your home.

A messenger had brought the news about Richard just this morning, carrying a letter of regret and slender hope to his mother from the army chaplain, who was Richard's cousin. The battle where he'd been wounded had been a week ago, and Martine, his mother, had assumed that he must be dead by now. She collapsed in a wailing heap in the village square, and Christine and her sister Laurel had helped to carry the grieving woman home.

Everyone had given up on Richard. Everyone, that is, except Christine.

She had come home for a week's leave to get a respite from the battle and the horrible sights that she had seen. Respites like this were occasioned only when the things the nurses had seen and endured would have been enough to make grown men go pale. Nurses who came home on leaves like this often failed to return to their duties, and no doubt people were expecting that she would stay home, too. In truth, she had considered it. But that was before the letter, and before she knew beyond question what she had to do.

The messenger, a messenger from the army, had agreed to meet her only after hours of harassment. He said that he would meet her here in the ruins of St. Agnes and that he would take her back with him to the sector where the battle had been fought. He had promised, and she wondered now if he had lied. The church was not large, and it had been made smaller by the piles of broken stone and wood. No army messenger was waiting for her that she could see.

Laurel had told her she was being foolish, that there was no way the messenger was going to take a woman to the front. Christine was angry to see that her older sister was probably right, but she refused to give up so easily. She would wait. The messenger was probably delayed, or he was still drinking in Lamarque's pub. He would come. She just had to be patient. She would wait until dawn if she had to.

Another puff of wind blew through the shell hole in the wall, and the dry leaves scattered through the nave again, the only other congregants in the sanctuary tonight. She could hear the not-so-distant guns thumping away, and she could see the flashes of light on the horizon that showed where the armies kept pummeling each other. They fired those big guns night and day, reducing the world to a morass of noise and hammering. The din was a constant companion these days, and it seemed that the German guns were coming closer. It was a stray shell that had killed St. Agnes' Church, and that was far too close for comfort. Most people had already gone, and the rest were leaving, if not tomorrow, then the next day. Her own mother and sister were leaving with a wave of refugees in the morning, heading south and away from the contending armies.

Let them run. Christine was heading north.

A crunching sound near the blasted wall grabbed her attention, and she turned to face the sound with a pounding heart, hoping against hope that the army messenger had come at last. She clutched her nurses' bag before her as if the bandages and medicines she carried would be protection against an attack if one should come. She saw the peak of a helmet as its wearer climbed over the rubble, but this was not the man she had expected. He was an infantry soldier, his horizon blue overcoat splattered with mud. His blue trousers were tucked into puttees that wound around his lower legs from knee to ankle, and these, like his boots themselves, were more mud than uniform now. The brown leather belt over his coat was scuffed but serviceable, and his bearded face had the drawn look she had come to recognize. This man was exhausted, and possibly in pain.

Christine rushed forward. "*Monsieur*, how can I help you?"

For a moment, he seemed bewildered, looking around the church as if he wasn't expecting to see it there. With shaking hands, he took a pipe from one of his belt pouches and put it between his teeth. There was no tobacco in the bowl, and he made no move to fill it. He merely stood there, clenching the stem, his fair eyes flickering across the shattered stones until they came to rest upon her face.

He looked surprised. "*Mademoiselle.*"

She carefully approached. Sometimes the least motion could make a shell-shocked soldier erupt in fear or violence. She'd seen it happen before. He watched her blankly, and she slowly, gently put a hand on his forearm. His coat sleeve was cold from being outside in the wind.

"Are you hurt?"

He blinked, then removed his helmet, revealing a shock of flaxen hair. He raised it to her as if he was doffing his cap. "I am Pierre Lausanne," he greeted, his voice soft. She thought she heard music in it and wondered if he sang. "I... I was sent."

"Sent?"

He put the helmet back upon his head. "To retrieve you, *mademoiselle*. For Richard. He asks for you."

Her heart leaped into her throat. He was alive! She gripped the man's arm. "Oh, thank you! Yes!

Take me to him. Is he in a field hospital, or better, behind lines?"

The guns spat, and Lausanne's eyes flickered toward the noise. He shook his head. "No. But I was sent to take you to him if you will come."

"Of course I'll come," she said eagerly. "Lead the way."

Lausanne hesitated, looking up at the crucifix. "I wonder," he said softly.

She followed his gaze. "What do you wonder, sir?"

"I wonder if He will look like that when I finally get to see Him."

Christine bit her lip. "I suppose it all depends upon what you believe."

He turned to her. His eyes seemed as if he were looking at her from a hundred miles away instead of standing at her side. He was distant, and she had seen that expression on dozens of faces before.

"Do you need to sleep before we go?" she asked. She didn't want to wait, but the man was exhausted, clearly about to fall asleep standing up.

He shook his head. "No. There isn't enough time."

Lausanne turned and walked away, leaving Christine to follow him. He walked at a steady pace, something she might not have thought him capable of after seeing the fatigue in his eyes, and she found herself scurrying to keep up. He looked back once to see that she was following, and then he began to walk.

She trailed him down the road, leaving the village behind and venturing into the darkness. Only the flashes of the guns illuminated the path. The moon was concealed behind heavy clouds, a combination of rain and gun smoke, and it was difficult to see. She knew this lane, but in the dark, with the thumping artillery and the strangeness of the man who was escorting her, Christine felt afraid.

Lausanne led her to a fork in the road where two horses stood, waiting but not tethered. One of them kept its head down, sagging with bone-numbing fatigue all its own, but the other looked up when they approached. It whickered to them, offering them a friendly greeting. These horses had been taken from their homes and pressed into service, dragging heavy guns and loads of shells. Somehow, this horse still found it in its heart to not hate humans. Christine wasn't certain she could say the same.

There were no saddles on the horses, but she had ridden bareback all her life. One didn't grow up in a farming village without knowing how to do such things. She and Richard had once taken her father's plow horses and ridden them all the way to the orchards outside Paitiens, the next town over, where they'd had a leisurely picnic in the sun. That had been the summer before the war.

She allowed Lausanne to help her onto the back of the livelier horse. His hands were firm and cool at her waist, and she thought about all of the men at the front with no shelter from the weather. They must all have been frozen through and through. Christine settled on the horse's back and took its chestnut main in her hand, the other hand gripping her bag to her torso lest it fall. Lausanne swung up onto the other horse, and then he led the way back down the road again.

The horses' hooves clopped quietly in a syncopated rhythm as they proceeded single file down the road. The guns flashed, and Christine's mount swiveled its ears back in dismay, but it continued on its course. The poor exhausted beast that Lausanne rode did not react.

Christine thought back to that picnic in the sun. They'd eaten chicken pies and drank red wine that Richard had taken from his mother's pantry. They'd shared apples and conversation, and she remembered Richard reciting bawdy poetry that he had learned at school. How she'd blushed at the things those rhymes depicted, and to hear them in her Richard's voice? Scandal. But she'd also laughed, hiding her giggles behind her hand, and Richard had laughed along with her, his dark eyes sparkling.

His eyes were her favorite part of him, she thought. They were always filled with intelligence and sparkling with mischief. They were dark, like the eyes of a doe, and when he kissed her they were filled with so much love it made her melt inside. She remembered when he'd looked at her that way during that picnic, and it made her miss him all the more.

There had been another picnic, one that had taken place during the last harvest festival their town had celebrated. It was hard to believe that it had already been two years since that blissful day. Richard, who attended school in Paris, had returned for the festival, and he'd been hard at work in the field beside his brothers, bringing in the wheat. Christine and her sister Laurel worked with the other young women, tying up the sheaves and preparing the meal for the hungry men. Their families had been neighbors all their lives, and they often worked together at harvest time. Laurel and Richard's brother David were keeping company, and everybody knew that one day they'd be married. The same was said of Christine and Richard, and neither of them disputed that thought.

She'd tucked some food away into a basket, and when Richard came to get a drink and take a moment's reprieve from the hard work, she'd spirited him away to the oak grove behind her father's barn. The leaves had all turned to gold, and most were still on the tree that glorious October day. She spread the blanket beneath the spreading limbs, and they'd eaten together, enjoying the warmth of the breeze and the dappled sunlight that fell upon their faces.

She could remember the moment as if it was still happening. Richard, his dark eyes soft and warm with emotion, gazing at her. His hand gently touching the curling tendril of hair that had fallen from her bun to bounce beside her cheek. His lips soft when they'd touched hers. She had put her arms around him, returning his sweet kiss, and he had pulled her close, laying her back upon the blanket until they were lying in one another's arms.

She'd known that he desired her, and the proof of it pressed against her hip. The feeling of it roused heat within her that she had never felt before, and she knew that if she burned, it was for him. He'd touched her waist, skimming along the bones of her corset until he brushed the soft mound of her breast. She'd never been touched that way before, and the moment had made her gasp in surprise at the pleasure it caused.

"My darling," he had whispered, looking down into her eyes. "I will marry you someday. When I graduate from school and come back for you, will you accept me then?"

It had seemed like such a long time to wait, but she knew that she would wait for him until Judgment Day. "Oh, yes," she'd promised. "Richard, I accept you now."

He'd kissed her deeper, his tongue touching hers, his hands stroking her in ways that made her heart pound out of her chest. She had reveled in that touch, and she gloried at the moment when his weight settled down on top of her, his knee sliding between hers. His breath had quickened, and the expression in his eyes had stunned her almost into insensibility. She had never known that desire could be worn so plainly.

But when he began to lift her skirt, she stopped him. They were not yet wed, and she was still too young. Her hand had caught his wrist, stilling his motion, and though he groaned, he obeyed. Richard had let her skirt lay where it was, and they contented themselves with kisses, both yearning for that other connection that would come someday.

She wished now that she hadn't stopped him.

Hours later, in the dark hour just before dawn, they were still riding. Lausanne nudged his horse, and the tired animal turned toward the right, following a sloping road that was covered over with fallen leaves. The scent of autumn's decay rose as the horses' hooves crushed and scattered the rotting vegetation, but the scent was tinged with a different sort of stench. Decay, indeed, was the odor wafting toward her now, and she knew that they were coming closer to the battlefield.

The war was being fought so close to where they lived. The whole of northern France had been turned into a killing field. The trenches that had been dug a year ago still stood, still manned. The lines had not moved at all, but the fighting had continued. Artillery rained hell down upon the men living like rabbits in their warren. Sometimes a general would send the men "over the top," ordering them to charge into barbed wire barricade and the spitting bullets of machine gunfire. The generals believed wholeheartedly in the *élan* of the French troops, but even the fighting spirit of the men was not enough to stop hot lead. So many men had died in this folly, and there were so many deaths to come.

Lausanne turned and whispered, "We will leave the horses now. The terrain is dangerous. Can you go on foot?"

"Yes," she answered instantly. She would walk into the fires of Hell if it meant seeing her Richard again.

Lausanne nodded and slid from his weary horse's back, and Christine left her mount, as well. They tethered the animals to a broken wagon and proceeded toward the front.

The smell of the trench was getting stronger now, the stench of open latrines and unwashed men and corpses left to rot in the open air combining into a choking miasma. She covered her mouth and nose with her hand until Lausanne looked back at her, and then, ashamed, she dropped her hand back to her side. If Richard and this brave fellow had survived for months breathing this unwholesome air, then she could bear it for a night.

They reached the trench, and she was shocked to find that it was empty. A massive shell had fallen directly on the scar scratched into the earth, and she could see where the walls of the ditch had collapsed. A hand, black with decay, stuck out of the pile of mud, and she turned away. Everywhere she looked it was the same: the trench destroyed, filled in with mud that had been flung by the explosions, and dead men lying where they'd died.

Christine crossed herself and turned to Lausanne, who stood staring at the carnage with a blank expression on his face. "Is Richard here?" she asked, choking on tears she was trying not to shed. "Did he die here? Was the message wrong?"

He stared into the trench as if he had not heard her, his gaze locked upon the booted feet of some poor man who had been shattered by the bomb. His legs were there, but the rest of him was gone. She wondered if it was someone Lausanne knew.

"*Monsieur*," she said, trying to get his attention. "*Monsieur?*"

Lausanne's pale eyes swiveled up to meet her face. "Richard is not yet dead," he answered her at last, "but he will die if he's not soon found."

Christine scrambled through the bloody muck and grabbed his coat. "Then take me to him!"

Lausanne looked into the trench once more, then nodded his head. "Come with me."

There was a place where the trench wall had collapsed and formed a kind of ramp, and it led up to the top of the wall and the edge of the battlefield. He led her there, stepping into the mud that sucked their feet in up to mid-calf. She struggled to free herself, nearly falling into the muck when her best effort resisted all attempts to extricate her legs. Lausanne took her hand firmly and pulled her free. She grimaced at the squelching sound the earth made when it released her, and the thought of being trapped there forever with all those slaughtered men made her shiver.

In no man's land, stakes were stabbing out of the ground like treacherous weeds, snarled with barbed wire that connected them in a rusting iron tangle. Lausanne hesitated at the edge of the expanse, facing the German trench that still stood opposite them. She didn't know if there were still soldiers there or not. The air felt unnaturally still, even though the artillery kept firing, and the flashing preceded the *whoomp* sound of the shells falling down like malicious rain. If there was a Hell, then this place was part of it.

Lausanne turned and nodded to her. "I will take you out to him, but stay low to the ground. They will shoot you if they see you."

She nodded, trying to will her hands not to shake. She had brought her nursing bag, but now she feared that the supplies might not be enough. She clutched it to her chest again.

He looked out at the German trench again, then gave a sigh that sounded like his heart was breaking. Christine wondered how many of his friends lay lost out in the space between the Germans and their own French troops, and how many of the bodies they had already passed had belonged to people known to him.

She would never ask. Some questions had answers too terrible to be spoken.

Lausanne stayed between her and the Germans the whole way. He grabbed some of the barbed wire and pushed it down with his hands, lowering it so that Christine could step over the thorny obstacle as if it were a country style. Her skirt caught on the wire, and she struggled to get it loose. In the rare quiet of the hesitation between shells, the fabric ripped, and the tearing sound was loud in Christine's ears. She was certain that the enemy had heard her, and she held her breath. Lausanne stayed still, blocking her from the German trench with his body, but no shots rang out, and she blew out nervously. She gathered up her skirts in her hand, holding them at the level of her thighs and stepped over the wire, leaving modesty behind. She was certain Lausanne had other things to think about than the way she had exposed her legs to him.

They crept that way for what felt like hours, stepping over the wire when they could push it down. There were more corpses here, some hanging in the wire that they passed, and Lausanne tried to keep himself interposed between Christine and the worst of the sights, but he could not conceal it all. She was shaken to her soul by what she saw.

They finally made it past the first bank of barbed wire obstacles, out into a ten-foot-wide expanse that was riddled with holes left by exploding shells. The holes were wet, half-filled with stinking green-brown water and the bodies of fallen soldiers. The guns' flashes were brighter now, and when they fired, she could see the alien landscape of death and ruin all around them. Her Richard was here, somewhere.

"How much further?" she asked Lausanne in a whisper.

He looked. "Not far." He pointed. "There. Do you see?"

"I don't see him."

The soldier took her hand in his. His grip was like ice. "Come this way."

They went faster now since the wire was gone, but she stumbled frequently over what she told herself were branches in the muck. The rainclouds that had been glowering all night opened up, and it began to pour.

Lausanne steered her toward a deep hole that she could smell before she ever saw it. Dead men floated face down in a brackish puddle, their gore adding to the sickly mud and clay. She saw several more men, huddled together and with their faces turned down toward the ground. The whole thing smelled of death.

"In there?" she asked, horrified.

"Yes," Lausanne told her. "He is there."

"But…"

"Go in."

She screwed up her courage and forced herself to step forward. The earth seemed to reach up toward her, grabbing her legs and pulling her down. She struggled just to take another step, then turned to face Lausanne.

He was gone.

Christine wanted to call out for him, but she knew that if she raised her voice, the Germans troops would hear and that could be her death. As it was, the flash of the cannons exposed her, and she heard the rat-a-tat of rifle fire. She flung herself onto her face, flattening her body into the mud, and the bullet soared over her. One struck the nurse's bag where it had landed beside her face, and she let out an involuntary shriek of fear.

Ahead of her, someone stirred. Amid the huddled pile of men, a white hand fluttered. A man's arm was straining through the stack of corpses, and she knew without a doubt that it was Richard.

There was no logic behind the feeling, but she let the conviction overtake her, and it brought courage with it. Christine pushed herself up out of the mud and down toward the ghastly scene. The white hand flapped again, striking against the back of a fallen *poilu*. She heard a gurgling cry.

"Help me..."

Praying for strength and speed, she pushed herself to move. She crossed the rest of the shell hole and its roiled mud until she was standing by the wounded man buried beneath his dead companions.

"Hold on," she said. "I've come to help you."

He moaned, and Christine marshaled all of her strength and determination to pull the corpses away from him. They were heavy, but she was strong both from working on her father's farm and transferring patients in the hospital. The rain both helped and hindered, making the corpses slippery enough to slide out of the way, but making the ground a bitter soup that tried even harder to suck her down.

She tried to focus on the hand, taking as little note as she could of the horrors all around. She was lost in a nightmare, and for the first time, she doubted whether this was really Richard at all. It didn't matter. This was a man who needed help, and she was a nurse and she was here. Whoever he was, French or German or English, it didn't matter. He was still a man, and by God, she would help him.

She pulled the last of the dead men away, revealing the face she had been hoping to see. Richard blinked up at her in feverish amazement, his dark eyes glinting.

"Christine? Can it be you?"

She kissed him, hard, and then pulled away to evaluate his wounds. He had been shot several times, but none of the wounds in themselves were likely to threaten his life. The threat to his life was in the diseased water all around him, and in the downpour that was filling the hole still deeper.

"Can you stand?" she asked.

"My leg..."

He had been shot in the thigh, but low, and the blood had clotted and closed the awful wound at least in part. She thought perhaps to bandage it, but that would trap infection inside, and she needed to get it clean.

"I see," she nodded. "What about the other leg?"

He was bewildered and in shock, and his mind was foggy, but he tried the limb in question. It bent agreeably.

"It was held down," Richard told her. "I was pinned…"

"I've moved them. We need you to stand. I can't carry you by myself."

Richard, now freed from the weight that had been holding him in the mud, managed to get his good leg beneath him. The motion made him white with pain, but he kept moving, and Christine gave him as much support as she could, wrapping his arm around her neck. Together they got him up onto his one strong foot.

He winced and bit his lip against the agony he was feeling, and Christine's heart broke for him, but they battled against his injuries together. She half-supported, half-carried him up the side of the shell hole, leaving the carnage he had been lying in behind. The guns flashed, revealing a section of no man's land that seemed dryer than the rest, and she thought she saw Lausanne along that path, beckoning for them to follow.

They made their slow and painful way out of the hole, and when the guns flashed again, Christine held her breath. They were standing too tall, and they would be shown too clearly to any gunman who happened to be watching. The first time it happened, the Germans did not respond, and she managed to get Richard halfway to where Lausanne was waiting.

They were not as fortunate a second time. The guns flashed, and for a split second the sky was bright as day, and Christine found herself staring into the eyes of a German soldier. Their path had taken them near the lip of the enemy trench, and they had somehow passed through a gap in the wire. She hadn't realized how close they'd come.

The soldier's rifle lifted, the muzzle pointing at them. Christine held her breath.

Richard wheezed out a sentence in a language she didn't know, and she realized that he was speaking German. She was stunned until she remembered that he had studied that language in his university. The soldier in the trench responded, then slung his rifle over his shoulder and scrambled out of the trench.

Christine's heart pounded in panic as the enemy soldier approached. He grabbed Richard's other arm, and her lover cried out for the first time. The German soldier grinned at her and spoke in heavily-accented French.

"Pretty girl."

He put Richard's arm over his shoulder, and he helped her carry her wounded soldier to a German ambulance that stood nearby. The horses were still hitched up, but there were no drivers around them. It seemed that all of the soldiers in the area were sleeping, and she wondered if there was some sort of miracle at play.

The soldier helped her put Richard on a stretcher in the back of the ambulance. He pointed at her bag and then at Richard, then grinned at her and patted her on the shoulder. He went away shouting.

She was certain that they were about to be captured, or worse, but she did the only thing she knew. She opened her bag and found alcohol and bandages, a syringe, and a single vial of morphine. He was suffering; she could see it in his eyes. His eyes had always spoken so clearly to her before. She reached for the morphine.

Richard grabbed her wrist. "No," he said. "Leave me awake."

"But…"

"We still have too far to go. Please." He smiled for her. "I can bear it."

The thumping sound of boots came from the front of the ambulance, and then a German voice – the voice of the soldier who had helped them – spoke. Richard sagged with relief.

"What is it?" she asked. "What did he say?"

Richard brought her hand to his lips. "We're safe, my love."

She couldn't imagine using that word now, but he seemed both sincere and grateful. The ambulance lurched forward, and she prayed to every saint she'd ever heard of that they would indeed make it to a hospital where he could get some care.

The ambulance rumbled along the track, jostling as the soldier took them faster than the hour and the conditions of the road should have allowed. She didn't know how long they drove. She only knew that she was with her man, and he was alive, and his bright eyes were locked with hers the entire way.

Dawn found them at a French field hospital, where their German driver surrendered as a prisoner of war. The doctors pulled Richard's stretcher out of the ambulance, and they rushed him to the surgical tent while one of the matrons pulled Christine aside. The older woman delivered a lecture, but Christine didn't hear a word of it.

She was taken to the nurses' quarters, where she was put into a bath and given fresh clothes. The stench of the dead men and the water they'd been lying in clung to the uniform that she had been wearing, and she was happy to relinquish them.

The clothes they gave her were a simple traveling dress, not the nurse's uniform she had expected. The matron came into the tent with a mug of tea, and Christine gestured to the skirt as she was dressing.

"Am I not going to be working?"

The matron looked at her as if she'd lost her mind. "No. You are dismissed."

"Dismissed?"

"Breaking too many regulations." The matron pulled herself up to her full, unimpressive height. "No woman is to set foot upon the battlefield or near those trenches, no matter what the reason."

She was stunned. "Oh…"

"Besides," the matron continued. "You have all the nursing you can handle with that man you brought in here. He'll need someone to care for him. His war is over, and you're both being evacuated back to Paris."

Christine gaped at her.

The older woman clicked her tongue. "Now, finish dressing, drink this tea, and come with me. Your man is waiting."

She did as she was told. She was put into a tent with an empty cot, deposited into a folding chair to wait while Richard's surgery went forward. She found herself dozing, too exhausted to stay awake. The efforts of the night before had left her drained, and not even the sounds and bustle of the hospital were enough to keep her from falling asleep.

Christine was awakened when she heard Richard cough. Her eyes snapped open, and she saw him lying in the cot, his face frighteningly pale. He was sleeping, and she gently pressed the back of her hand to his forehead. He had a fever, but not a bad one, and she counted that as good luck.

She looked down at his sleeping form and saw that luck of a different kind had also been to visit him while she was sleeping. His left arm was missing at the elbow now, and the stump was bandaged right. She saw now why the matron said that his war was done.

Christine's eyes filled with tears, and she got down on her knees beside the cot. She folded her hands and bowed her head in thanks, grateful that he had been spared, and that he would not be risked on the front again. She doubted that he would be as happy about the loss of his arm, but she blessed the infirmity because it meant that she could keep him home.

He spoke in a whisper, interrupting her prayers. "You came all this way for me?"

She looked up into his handsome face, into those gleaming brown eyes that she had loved for years. "I would go anywhere for you."

Richard smiled, and she bent to kiss him. His lips were scratchy with whiskers, and it tickled her face. She laughed.

"Brave, impetuous little fool," he gently chided. "You could have been hurt."

"You *were* hurt. I wasn't going to let you stay out there alone."

Richard shook his head. "How did you know I was injured?"

She took his remaining hand and held it, stroking her fingers over the strong, square shape of it. He had always had manly hands, and she would love him no less now that he was left with only one.

"A messenger came to the village with a letter from your cousin. He told your mother that you had been injured."

"How did she take it?"

Christine hesitated, then admitted, "Not well."

Richard nodded. "And here at the front… how did you know where to find me?"

"Ah! Well, one of your fellows brought me here."

"That was reckless of him, but I'm so very grateful. Did he give his name?"

She nodded. "He said his name was Pierre Lausanne."

Richard's eyes widened, but any response was forestalled by the appearance of the doctor and the chaplain, who was Richard's cousin.

The days that followed were filled with Richard's care. By order of the doctors, he was dosed with morphine and slept more than he was awake. The chaplain, Père Daniel, kept Christine company at Richard's bedside, watching over him when Christine slept or took her meals.

They were evacuated to Paris as the matron had said, and Père Daniel went with them. The apartment that Richard had rented while he was at school was still available, and they moved him back into those familiar settings.

Richard improved, and he never spoke of the war, not even when the sound of the guns reached them there in the capital. He spoke of apples and of the autumn leaves that fell from the tree outside their window. He spoke of how her reputation would suffer when people learned that she was staying there with him, and though he was teasing, she knew he was concerned for her and what people would say, so she asked Père Daniel if he would marry them. On a cold day in October, in the side chapel of Notre Dame, they were wed. Christine gave herself to him with joy that night, and after Richard became the first and last lover in her life, they slept in one another's arms.

She rose the morning after their wedding to begin their first day as man and wife. Richard reclined in the bed and watched her as she brushed her hair. She smiled at him and blushed.

"You're staring."

"So I am." He smiled and looked down at his stump. "I'm so blessed that you would still have me."

Christine put her brush aside and returned to their marriage bed. "I told you that I would accept you, and I do. I will love you until the end of time, no matter how many arms you have." She kissed him. "It's your heart that matters. Your soul."

"Speaking of souls…" He looked away.

"What is it?"

"You said that Pierre Lausanne led you to me."

She nodded. "Yes. I was thinking we should ask Père Daniel to say a mass in his honor, out of gratitude."

Richard swallowed. "Did you… Could you describe Pierre Lausanne?"

Christine frowned. "About your height, blond hair, fair eyes…"

He closed his eyes and his face went pale, and she grabbed his hand. "Richard? What's wrong?"

"Pierre Lausanne…" He took a breath. "I told him about you – and about our love. He said that he would have given anything to have such feelings in his own life. He swore… He swore that he would see to it that I lived to see your face again."

"And he did," she told him, giving him a warm smile. "He took me to you."

He swallowed hard and looked into her eyes.

"Pierre…he was an honest man. He died two days before I was injured..."

The End

About the Author

J. A. Cummings was born in Flint, Michigan and was raised in a nearby town called Clio. Appropriately enough for someone growing up in a place named for the Muse of history, she developed a passion for reading and the past that continues to this day. Her love of poetry and storytelling quickly followed.

Her life has been one of numerous false starts, unexpected endings, and fascinating side trips that lasted far too long. All of that chaos has informed her writing and improved her understanding of what it means to be human, both the sorrow and the glory. She still resides in Michigan.

The Farm in the Forest
By Nichole Craig

Zachariaz runs a farm. Unlike other ordinary farms, you won't find chickens and cows. On his mythological creature farm, every day can seem repetitive, but with one misstep, everything can come crumbling down.

The keychain felt heavier today, we must have gotten new creatures. New creatures appear a lot, I haven't figured out how they know how to find the farm. The barns aren't too far from the house; but far enough that I've considered on more than one occasion building a horse stable next to the house. I haven't done it because we don't keep horses, I think some of the creatures would be offended if we did.

    I take care of the barns alone four days out of the week, the other days I have workers to help out. The first barn I stop at only looks like a barn on the outside, inside it is a fully furnished two-story apartment. Inside are creatures that come and go as they please. They have their own sets of keys to their individual rooms. We have a maid service for them twice a week, but I still check on a few close friends even on my days off.

    My first stop inside the barn is the first room. Sliban isn't the messy sort but if he drops something he can't pick it up. I knock on his door and hear him yell, "come in" taking my keys out I unlock the door.

    "Ah Zachariaz, good day! I expect you slept well?" Sliban asks.

    "I did, thank you. Did the soundproofing I added to Daralds room work?"

    "It helped tremendously."

    "Can I get you anything? A blanket maybe? It's getting cold." His naked chest is eye level to me, I've offered him shirts in the past but he is never interested. I look around his room, he doesn't have a bed he sleeps standing up. His bookshelf is getting full, I make a mental note to make him another.

"That's alright I enjoy the breeze but if you could, I seemed to have dropped this book, just at a good part too." He kicks it.

He has clumsy fingers, he can bend at his waist but can't exactly reach down and touch his hooves. I pick up his book and hand it to him.

"What happened to that device I gave to you for reaching?" I ask him.

"I dropped it," he said sheepishly, "It's there in the corner."

Smiling I pick it up and set it on his bookshelf.

"Let me know if there's anything else you need Sliban."

Sliban has been staying here for decades – since before I ran the ranch. My grandfather told me he is the last half-horse, half-man that he knows of. When I was younger I would sit with the centaur and he'd read to me.

I say my goodbyes to Sliban then close and lock the door behind me. The doors have specific locks to fit the creature. Daralds room only unlocks on the outside. Evadne and Samias's room lock only on the inside, they worry Roceq would try to pick the lock if there was one on the outside.

I head towards the second floor to check on Darald but stop when I see Roceq standing outside Evadne and Samia's room.

"Roceq if you continue to harass the nymphs, you're going to have to move on."

"They're not here, they just left to go frolic, I just like the smell of the hall after they leave," Roceq inhales.

I inhale, the hall smells of Iris and rain. "Nevermind their scent I'll get you a candle. You just need to stop being so creepy."

"It's just so hard; you can't understand. They are so beautiful," he sighs.

"Nymphs have no interest in any type of relationship, especially with a satyr. What happened to the girl you were talking to?"

"Fawns, man. She left me for a minotaur – like that's going to work out," He spits.

"Well, keep looking; your fawn is out there." I raise my voice a little, "Stop. Bothering. The. Nymphs."

Satyrs are perverted creatures, and being half-goat, half-human, I don't think even their own species finds them attractive.

I return making my way up the stairs. Daralds room is the only one with a steel door. It's quiet in his room, but I did just install the soundproofing. I check to make sure I have my taser, Roceq tries to take it sometimes to try and fight minotaurs. Finding it at my hip, I tense as I unlock and open Daralds door.

I immediately relax when I walk in. Past out on the floor lays Darald. He's naked like I always find him in his human form. I go to his scratched up dresser and find him some clothes, I turn around to set them on his bed but find his bed all tore up. I let out a huff and throw them on it anyway. Finding the spray bottle on the counter somehow still intact I pick it up and spray Darald. Luckily the spray bottle stream reaches a good distance. He may be in human form, but anyone being woken up by spray bottle can get pretty angry.

Darald grumbles and stirs.

"Come on; time to get up, sleepyhead." I spray him again.

He looks up to me, confused.

Apparently, turning into a werewolf for a week and back into a human scrambles your brain.

He's never hungry when he wakes but I offer to make him eggs anyway.

"I'll come down when you're done with your walkthrough," Darald finally says.

****

Lunchtime rolls around, and I go to work boiling harpy eggs. The eggs have a spice to them that chicken eggs don't.

Darald walks in, this time fully dressed and sits down at the old creaky table.

"Did the soundproofing work?" he asks sleepily.

I put a cup of coffee in front of him, "Sliban had no complaints."

"Sliban never has any complaints,".

I look over to him, after wolfing out he always needs a shave and a haircut, but the rough look suits him.

"You're right," I laugh, "No one else said anything."

Wolfing out is a painful experience for Darald and I imagine other werewolves. It starts with him screaming in agony and ends with him screaming in agony. In between, he howls and growls, tearing up everything in his path. I imagine Darald is the only werewolf in Poland because unlike other countries, no villages have been reported destruction by wolf-like beasts. At least not since the massacre of the werewolves.

"Would you like any hard-boiled harpy eggs or pig wings?" I ask him

"Just a splash of gold milk for my coffee," he pauses "if we have any."

Gold milk is intoxicating and sweet. I pour some into his coffee, "You need to convince Roceq to get some more from the sheep."

"I can be persuasive," He winks at me.

I smile at him. It's very hard to milk a golden sheep. For some reason she likes Roceq, probably has something to do with their breed similarities.

"Zaaach! Zaaaach!" I hear Roceq bah from outside.

Darald and I both rush to look out the screen door.

Roceq stops at the porch, hyperventilating, "Morrios-," he pauses trying to catch his breath, "Morrios released all the creatures."

Darald begins to snarl and runs out the door nearly knocking down Roceq in his wake. The name sounds familiar, why would anyone release the creatures? I rush to the gun cabinet and grab my tranquilizer gun. I run after Darald but can't keep up with him. As I'm running I place the name, I can hear Roceq a distance behind me. I stop and take in the damage while I wait for him to catch up.

Darald is protecting creatures from the more aggressive ones kept in other barns. His snarling keeping them back for now. I aim the tranquilizer and shoot at an Ogre going after a hippogriff. I reload and shoot the ogre again, three times my size the ogre drops denting the ground. The hippogriff pecks the ogre with its beak, then gallops away jumping into the air he tucks his hooves under himself and flies away. He will come back hippogriffs are loyal creatures.

Already reloaded, I aim at a Harpy trying to swoop off with the golden sheep. Before I could shoot a pegasus bucks up shooing the harpy. The pegasus looks to me.

"Don't let the Harpies go anywhere, see if you can get them into their cage," I tell her.

The pegasus whinnies in response and flies off after the Harpies.

I look to Roceq who is watching the events unfold. "What happened to Morrios?"

"Sliban chased him off."

"What did you do to him to piss him off?"

"I did nothing, Minotaurs are just hot-headed."

Darald calls over to us, "What of the Dragon?"

I feel the color leave my face and my heart begins to race, I forgot about the dragon.

"He didn't make it over there," Roceq says.

The Nymphs appear dancing around the creatures, "Hello Zachariaz," one of them sings.

"Hello, Darald," the other sings.

The animals begin to calm. I can't tell them apart, they're twins, or all Nymphs look alike, I'm not sure.

Their beauty is flawless, men can't resist them, well most men. Their skin is a very deep blue, and their hair is golden, long enough to fall past their waist if they stood still. They dance and sing with everything they do.

"Hey Evadne, and Samia, Do you girls think you can get the creatures to return to their pens?" I ask them.

"Surely, they are happier in the sun," one of them sings.

"Just like we are," the other sings and jumps in the air.

"You know they all get their time in the sun but you don't want any of them to die because of the more aggressive ones do you?" I counter.

"You are right," one sings.

"We will help," the other sings.

"First, me must tell you of the human," she spins around the other.

"He was so cute, but we didn't dance with him like you said," sings the other.

"What human?" I say, looking around.

"In the forest," she sings.

"We heard Morrios and danced away," the other spins.

"I'll take care of the human," I tell them.

They prance to the doors as the creatures follow. Each going into their proper pen.

The hippogriff returns and assists pegasus with the harpies. Herding them into their cage. Darald and I drag the ogre to his cave-like prison. Dropping him on the floor with a thud.

"That's all of them," Roceq says following behind us every step of the way.

Darald Snarls, "What did you do to Morrios?"

"I guess he got a little mad when I told the fawn he's dating about another fawn he's seeing." Roceq shrugs.

"He's with a deer?" Darald asks.

"Female satyr," I explain.

"What are we going to do about the human? Shouldn't Sliban be back?" Darald asks.

"Grab a unicorn we will go look for him. We have to make sure nothing happens to the human. If something does it will just bring more out this way," I tell him

"You guys can't go after a minotaur!" Roceq exclaims.

"We're not, we're going after Sliban, be useful, go clean the creatures' pens." Darald growls.

****

Following the dented brush Darald and I ride into the forest on the unicorns. Hearing commotion off the beaten path, the unicorns don't need to be directed. Unicorns are peaceful creatures unless you mess with one of their own, and though he's a different species they wouldn't want anything to happen to Sliban. I can tell the Unicorn Darald is riding is disgusted by his species.

We hear Sliban before we see him, "You had no right to disturb those creatures."

"I was looking for the little Satyr, my love left me because of him," Morrios growled.

Sliban and Morrios are standing in a small clearing, in the dense forest. I get off the unicorn.

"Then you shouldn't have cheated, my farm shouldn't suffer because you can't keep it in your umm-" I stop, unsure what the giant, bull-like creatures keep 'it' in.

Morrios interrupts my pondering, "Minotaurs are not monogamous."

"Well then you should have informed your girlfriends, communication is key."

This isn't what he wanted to hear, Morrios begins to scrape the ground with his hooves preparing to attack. Darald jumps in front of me as Morrios charges but Sliban pushes us both out of the way.

I look up to Sliban, who is blocking my view of Morrios. He didn't have time to fend off Morrios's attack. The point of one Morrios horn appears through Sliban's abdomen. The unicorns immediately run at Morrios spearing him on both sides of his chest killing him.

No way to catch him I jump out of the way as Sliban falls to the ground. I look over to Darald who must have gotten knocked out when Sliban pushed us out of the way. Looking around I lock eyes with a human, hiding in the brush. I go to Sliban, he's still breathing.

"Go get the Nymphs," I yell to the unicorns.

Sliban coughs, "No, it's time for me to be with my own kind."

"The Nymphs can help you!" I yell at him.

"The damage is much too great," he says, "take care of your own, this farm is just what all the creatures need."

We stare at each other, for what seems like forever, I can't think of one thing to say. Even after he passes out from blood loss, even after the nymphs arrive and inform me he's gone, I find nothing to say.

Not the time for tears, I turn to where the human stood. He's gone. I look down to Darald still knocked out cold, so much for a tracker.

"Evadne, and Samia, where did you see the human first?"

"A camp to the east," one sings, though for the first time I've ever seen not dancing around.

"The fires sang a beautiful tune," the other sings, tears in her eyes.

I walk east, the hoofbeats behind me telling me a unicorn is following behind.

"Don't get to close, I don't want the human to see you," I command it.

I smell the smoke first. When I come to a clearing with a tent and what's left a fire, I look around. The fire was doused, at least he had the sense to put it out. It hadn't been long since I saw him hiding so he has to be near to have time to come back to his camp.

"I don't want trouble. I don't know what I saw but I will chalk it up to bad berries. Just leave," the human says, coming out from behind his tent. He must've heard me approach and hid.

"Let me escort you back to town. If you ate bad berries you should seek medical help," I tell him.

Fear crosses his face when his eyes wander behind me. He snaps his gaze back to me. I look behind, where a unicorn stands. Horn bloodied. I scowl at the unicorn.

"Sit down, restart the fire, Let me tell you a tale," I tell the man.

The man nervously restarted the fire, glancing up every few seconds to look at the unicorn. He is young, 15 or more years younger than me.

"You have a family?" I ask.

The man's eyes widen.

"I'm sorry. I don't mean you any harm," I say not realizing how threatening my question sounded.

"My girlfriend is pregnant. I'm only 17, I'm not ready to be a father. My father used to bring me to these woods when he was alive. I came here to think," he says.

He's younger than I thought, "When I was a boy 6 or 7, nearly 30 years ago, my grandfather ran the farm. A man wandered onto the farm and discovered it's secrets. The man went back to town and told others, they came, pitchforks and all, creatures fled scared. They wreaked havoc for weeks in town. Destroying crops, eating sheep or family pets. Don't get me started on what happened with the werewolves. The people in town came back to my grandfather asking him to fix it. With the help of a family friend, Sliban, they got the creatures back. The people in town agreed to never come this far or speak of it again. My grandfather was hesitant about this agreement. He had some Nymphs erase the townsfolk memory forget about that entire week. History repeats itself, future generations would get curious about the old tale not believing. They would come out here again. I have dangerous creatures you don't want to get out."

"Why are you telling me? I'm sure, like your grandfather, you will erase my memory," he says.

"Darald, the guy who was with me back there, he was turned into a werewolf when that happened. He was my age, the only thing we could do was take him in, away from his family. He was too young to understand, to control it. I can't have that happen again, to take a child from there family, and have them not know what happened, their memory was erased too you see. It haunts Darald," I keep my voice even.

He swallows tears in his eyes, "Before I was born, I had an Uncle who went missing as a boy. It left the town in an uproar, other unexplained things happened. Crops destroyed and animals missing overnight, no explanation as to why. My Uncle's name was Darald. My father was Darald's older brother."

I see Darald in him, his eyes, his untamed hair.

"I can't have-" I correct myself, "I won't be having any children, If the farm can't stay in my family it's only right it stays in Darald's family. Darald is family to me anyway. Come back to the farm with me. Let me show you it, if you don't think you can handle the responsibility then just please keep our secret. If you decide to take over there are plenty of rooms for you and your family. The house and farm will be all yours after I'm gone."

"Ok," he says, fear no longer in his eyes.

****

"What happened?" Darald sits up on the bed. I carried him back from the clearing while the unicorns took care of Sliban's body. I put the man, whose name I now know as Aleksander, in a room across the hall.

"You're home, Sliban didn't- he didn't make it, he saved us," I choke out.

"Oh, I'm so sorry Zachariaz," Darald motions for me to sit on the bed.

I sit down on the bed next to him. He pulls me into his arms. I lay on his chest. Darald stroking my hair. Sleep eventually takes me, but not soon enough.

About the Author

Nichole Craig is a writer, as you may have noticed. She has dabbled in a few genres, including sci-fi and paranormal. Though you won't see much of her work on the shelves, she has quite a few things written. She has two young children, a dog, and a husband. Netflix, cleaning, and video games are how she procrastinates from writing. Follow on Facebook @AuthorNicholeCraig.

Elle

By Alanna Robertson-Webb

Elle, a young woman on the run from supernatural entities, encounters a friend in an unexpected place. Will Ricky be able to help save his childhood friend, or will he lose her to a monster?

The ratty curtain began to pull back, the stage illuminated by flickering bulbs. The announcer's voice sounded dull and tired, a mirror of the men leering at the stage. This would be another night of seeing the same uninterested dancers perform, their minds on anything but the job they were getting paid to do.

The curtain opened, and for a moment the crowd's attention sharpened as they stared in confusion. The entire set up of this performer was new, including the fact that the curvy dancer was fully dressed and sitting on a chair. The young woman's hair was done up in a bun, and she sported the quintessential librarian look. Glasses, stockings, Mary Jane shoes, a plain white button-up shirt, and a black pencil skirt completed her unexpected ensemble. The announcer put a little pep in his voice, an instant signal that something interesting was happening, and he cleared his throat dramatically.

"And now, just for one night while she passes through town, I give you Candy Cannnnnnne! She looks sweet enough to lick, right gents?"

The announcer finished, and the Aurora song *Running with the Wolves* began to play. The crowd let out an unsure spattering of applause, their eyes unwaveringly drawn towards the unusual setup. While the music wasn't the typical upbeat hip-hop, and the dancer had way more clothes on than was expected, the attention of everyone in the room was magnetically attached to the stage.

Go row the boat to safer grounds
But don't you know, we're stronger now

My heart still beats and my skin still feels
My lungs still breathe, my mind still fears

But we're running out of time (time)
For the echoes in my mind cry

There's blood on your lies
Disguise opened wide
There is nowhere for you to hide
The hunter's moon is shining

I'm running with the wolves tonight
I'm running with the wolves
I'm running with the wolves tonight
I'm running with the wolves

Trick or treat, what would it be?
I walk alone, I'm everything
My ears can hear and my mouth can speak
My spirit talks, I know my soul believes

But we're running out of time (time)
For the echoes in my mind cry

There's blood on your lies
Disguise opened wide
There is nowhere for you to hide
The hunter's moon is shining

I'm running with the wolves

*I'm running with the wolves tonight
I'm running with the wolves
I'm running with the wolves tonight*

*It can cause betrayal, it hurts
I can't be dreaming
The night deceives us,
A million voices inside my dreams
My heart is left so incomplete*

*I'm running with the wolves
I'm running with the wolves*

With each stanza, a little more of her outfit came off, and soon she was down to a plain, white shift. She didn't dance, or move much, she just sat there reading while the rest of the song played. An occasional re-crossing of her legs made the crowd go wild, and when she shook her hair out of the bun, she saw multiple $20 bills land on the stage. The dancer ended the song by standing up, 'accidentally' dropping her book and bending over just long enough to show off a tiny bit of cleavage. The fact that she made any cash for doing virtually nothing baffled the regular strippers, but the young woman had learned long ago that classy equals sexy in these rural, tiny towns.

When she left the gentleman's club she was $478 richer, and she had enough money to be able to afford an actual hotel room for the night. She could even get a decent meal, while still having enough for a couple of bus tickets.

At least she hoped she would – if *they* didn't catch up with her first.

The young woman had initially found it easy to keep running, just doing one show every few nights to get the money that she needed, but she was getting tired from only sleeping in odd bursts before moving on. She knew that she couldn't keep her pace up forever, but she didn't know how to put an end to her living nightmare either. She needed to find a place with an authentic medicine man, and she was running out of time.

The strip club was on the edge of an abandoned highway that used to run through the center of an old prospecting town, but the area was now relatively rural save for the buildings she was passing by. As she walked along the cracked, old pavement she could hear her shoes thudding lightly, but they echoed in a way her steps shouldn't. She paid close attention, and soon caught the sound of a footstep that didn't manage to quite match hers. Every couple of minutes she would casually look around, her eyes scanning for her pursuer, but she saw nothing. There was a shadowed forest bordering the road, so if it came to it she would make a break for the treeline.

The row of buildings was coming to an end, the few, still-functioning street lights having ended about forty yards back. There was nothing but moonlight left to illuminate the sidewalk, and with the moon waning it was barely lighting up anything enough to see well. The dancer could sense that this was either where her pursuer would give up, or they'd jump her. The area was too far out for her to rely on help, so she placed her hand on the can of military-grade mace in her jacket pocket. She strode more briskly, and in her peripheral, she caught a glimpse of a figure leaving the final alleyway between the last two buildings.

It paused for a moment, as if unsure what to do, then it shouted for her.

"Hey, stop!"

She ignored it, her steps quickening until she was all but sprinting. She wasn't going to let the creatures catch up to her like this. She wanted to be where she could defend herself, even if she didn't stand much of a chance.

"Damnit Elle, wait!"

She skidded to a stop, her heels screeching against the concrete. Her pursuers didn't typically speak, so this had to be an actual person. The figure, which had sprinted after her, finally caught up. She faced it, spray raised and uncapped. Mustered her most intimidating voice Elle let out a gruff demand, her voice resonating clearly.

"What do you want?"

"I...uhnnn...damn, I'm out of shape...uggh."

The man was clutching his knees and panting, a self-deprecating chuckle escaping him. He straightened up after a moment, his hood still covering his face.

"I needed to know if it was you."

"Me?"

"Yeah. I know it's been a couple of years, but as soon as I saw you on stage I could tell it was you. You lost some weight, but otherwise, you look the same."

"Uh-huh. And you are...?"

He pulled his hood back, and even in the dim moonlight, Elle could recognize him. The wiry hair, the full-lipped grin, the same old type of sweatshirt that he sported back in highschool. It didn't matter that she couldn't make out the shape of his nose or see his beautiful, coffee-brown eyes. She knew instantly that it was her old best friend, and her heart did a little flip-flop.

"Ricky...?"

"Yup, in the flesh. Way to use Candy-Cane as your stage name, by the way. I didn't think you recalled me nicknaming you that back in 2012, but it looks like you remembered when you got sunburnt lines all over thanks to that stupid bathing suit you were wearing."

"I did. It's not like I could easily forget the one thing you teased me mercilessly about for the rest of that year."

"Of course not. You always were the smartest person I knew."

"You don't know how good it is to see a friendly face here. I really, really missed you, Ricky."

He flashed her a grin, and Elle wanted to cry.

Seeing him there, in person rather than in her dreams, made the walls she had worked so hard to build up crack a fraction. She had moved away from their childhood hometown a few years back and had lost touch with him when he stopped responding to her letters. She had been so mad at him, so hurt, but the relief she felt in that moment far outweighed any resentment she had harbored.

Without thinking she threw her arms around him, burying her face in the crook of his neck. It was the first physical contact she had had in a while, and it felt incredible. Ricky unhesitatingly wrapped his arms around her, and for just a second she felt like she had never left. She had missed him more than almost anyone, and she never wanted to let him go.

"Elle, what in Hell happened to you? We thought you were dead. Your mom had missed you so much, and I, well, I didn't want to give up hope, but when she called to see if you had come to stay with me...It hurt too much to stay there, knowing that you were missing. I wanted to do something to help, even a little, so I came here to see my dad. I thought that he might be able to hire a detective, but he's been away on business since Monday..."

She moved a step back, placing the mace can back in her pocket, but stayed within the circle of his arms. Craning her neck up she studied the shadows of face for a moment, and she wished that she had better light to read his expressions in.

"Did you say that she 'had' missed me?"

"Um, yeah…"

"What changed?"

Ricky took a breath. He never thought he was going to have to explain this to Elle, and he wasn't exactly prepared.

"This is gonna sound weird, but yesterday she was mauled to death by a really big dog – or a few of them. The cops weren't sure, and since it happened inside of her apartment they think a single dog is more likely. She was covered in fang marks and claw marks, so they know it wasn't a human who did it."

"It wasn't a dog."

Her response was so quiet that he would have missed it if she weren't face-to-face with him.

"What? How do you know that?"

"I can't explain it, but I have to go before they get you too..."

"Damnit Elle, stop talking in riddles! What trouble are you in? Who are you running from!?"

"I can't explain it."

"Can't, or won't?"

"Won't! You wouldn't believe me, no one does. That's why I need a shaman, someone who knows about things like them!"

"Try me."

Tears had started sliding down her cheeks, and Elle had begun trembling so hard that Ricky immediately drew her back against them. He felt her arms tighten around him as she choked back a sob, after a few moments she seemed to collect herself. She had never been a crier, and it didn't appear that she was going to start now. She shifted slightly so that she could run her fingers across his cheek, and her response held more anger in it than he would have thought possible.

"Werewolves, or some variant of them, are chasing after me. I'm going to kill them for what they did to her, and then you'll be safe. I can't stay; I don't want them to get your scent."

He stared at her, his expression lost in the shadows. He didn't say anything, but his embrace tightened slightly.

"How did it start?"

"I was in the woods, up in Sabin's Pasture behind the college. It was nighttime, and I had another fight with my mom so I went out to clear my head. I was near the ravine when one of them sprang out of the grass. It said something about blood knowing blood, and that I needed to join them and be free of my false mother. Of course, I freaked out, and I ran. They hounded me night after night, and I finally left because I found a note threatening my mom and the cats. I've been running since."

Without warning Ricky pulled her snugly against him, his chin resting against the top of her head. She was clearly mentally disturbed and didn't want to talk about whatever had actually happened to her. He would help her get back home, and make sure that she was okay. He could call up one of the local doctors and get her an appointment, and he'd be there to work through her trauma with her. There was nothing he wouldn't do to know she was safe.

"I know when you moved it was really tough, and I've wanted to see my best friend. I need to fix things, you know, with *us*. I missed you so much, but I didn't know how to say that. Then I freaked out and didn't respond to your letters because I didn't know how to explain what was going on in my head. Now you're here though, and I won't let you go again. You got that, El? You aren't going anywhere without me."

Ricky hadn't known she was missing, not until that phone call, and he was ashamed of himself. Now he had been given the chance to get her back, to see her smile again just for him, and he didn't have the words to say how happy that made him. Before Elle could respond a howl erupted behind them. It had come from back near the strip club, and it didn't sound like any dog that Ricky had ever heard.

"They're coming! It's me they want, so I'll distract them. You get inside!"

She yanked herself from him and started to run, refusing to heed his pleas to stop as he sprinted after her. She made it to the treeline, and as he was about to step off the sidewalk the sound of cracking branches and pounding paws erupted in front of them. Elle screamed, and she didn't have time to back up before something grabbed her wrist.

A hairy, gangly arm had shot out from behind the closest tree, and even in the minuscule light, Ricky could see that the fingers ended in claws instead of nails.

"What the fu...Elle, *no*! Shit!"

He lunged for her, his hand missing the back of her jacket by barely an inch. Ricky watched as her hair, the last thing he could see, disappeared past the treeline. He stood shock-still for a moment, his mind still trying to figure out if the whole scenario was a prank. A shudder skittered up his spine, and before he could overthink things he chased after her, his eyes adjusting to the dark just enough to keep him from tripping over anything. The fog was making it extra hard to see, but that didn't deter him.

He wasn't about to lose her again, even if this was a twisted joke.

Ricky could hear Elle up ahead, and it sounded like she was giving her attacker a tough time. She was screaming and cursing, and based on the occasional *thwack* it sounded like she was somewhat successful at hitting or kicking it. Vicious snarls and reverberating growls echoed around him, and it was all he could do to make himself run towards the danger. His instincts were humming, a keening vibration in his bones that told him this was wrong, and that right now he was the prey.

The thought of abandoning her briefly flitted across his consciousness, but he shoved that disgusting idea into the darkest recesses of his mind.

Ricky kept trying to rationalize that someone in a costume had dragged her off, but he had never known such shrill, terror-filled screams to come from Elle. She had never really been a trickster, and what few pranks she had ever pulled were funny or jerkish, not harmful or fear-inducing. Putting salt into her cousin's milkshake was one thing, but he knew that this was too surreal to be a joke.

His blind chase led him past hundreds of trees, their limbs leaving angry welts on his face as he shoved through the branches. Ricky couldn't see much, and after a few minutes, he realized that he could no longer hear anything.

"Elle, where are you!? Please, answer me!"

Silence.

Fear rolled through him in a nauseous wave. He had lost her. She was in these woods, with some kind of storybook monster, and he had failed to get her back. She could be dead, or still trying to get free, and he would have no idea. He strained his senses, but only the whistle of the wind reached him.

"Elle?"

His broken cry echoed eerily around the mist-clad forest, and he slumped to his knees. Mulch and cold mud oozed into his jeans, but he didn't care. Nothing mattered. Ricky could have saved her, he could have run a little faster, but he had hesitated. She was gone, and this time he didn't know how to bring her back.

About the Author

Alanna Robertson-Webb is a New York author who enjoys long weekends of LARPing, is terrified of sharks, and finds immense fun in being the chief editor at Eerie River Publishing.

She lives with a fiancée and two cats, all of whom like to take over her favorite cozy blanket when they think they can get away with it. She is currently an MRO support member by day and an editor and author by candlelight.

While she has been published before, which is wonderful, she one day aspires to run her own nerd-themed restaurant. Her work can be found on Amazon and her website here: https://arwauthor.wixsite.com/arwauthor.

Home to Heaven

By Jennifer Carr

Do you ever wonder if people can see loved ones who have passed away? My children are the only ones who know the answer to that question.

My children were the last people to ever see my grandma – and that was two years after her death.

We were attending my grandfather's funeral service when my 5-year-old son saw her.

My parents, siblings, husband, and kids were at the Johnson Funeral Home in Louisiana in honor of my grandfather who we grew up calling "Papa". He had peacefully passed on to the next life in his sleep.

That's the way I hope I die – peacefully in my sleep.

The funeral arrangements were made, and all his affairs were in order. We were having a Catholic mass with a few songs he had picked out before his death. During the service, the casket remained open. Papa was lying there peacefully in a basic grey suit and crisp white, button-up shirt and a buzz cut haircut. He looked just like he had my entire life.

We were all sitting in the pews. The atmosphere was somber and the priest was talking about his life in his eulogy. Nothing seemed out of the ordinary.

Then, all of a sudden, my then 7-year-old son bent over, started tugging at my black dress, and said, "Look! Who's that woman standing there next to the big box."

My mother and I both looked to where he was pointing. He was pointing towards the casket. We didn't see anyone.

"Where? What woman?" I asked my son.

He replied, "The one right there. She's wearing a blue flowery dress…"

We looked again and didn't see anyone near the casket. The priest was on the other side of the chapel at the pulpit and there was no-one remotely close to the casket.

We dismissed what he said and went back to listening to the service. Honestly, I had forgotten about *the woman*. Fast forward about an hour after the funeral, we were at the burial site. It was a simple but nice grassy area marked by a handsome gravestone with an airplane carved into it. Papa was in WW II as an airplane mechanic. Again, we were listening to the final words of the priest as the casket was being lowered into the ground.

This time, my 5-year-old daughter pulled at my dress. I looked down at her and she asked, "Who's that woman standing there?"

"Where?" I replied.

"There – looking into the ground," she said matter-of-factly.

I did not see anyone. "Where?" I asked her, bewildered.

"Right there – standing right there. She is looking in that hole in the ground. The lady in a pretty blue flower dress."

That made my head really turn around. The kids weren't even next to each other when my son saw the woman the first time and now my daughter was talking about her.

Puzzled, I wondered who this woman was that both my kids saw. I mentioned to my mom what the kids saw and where they saw her. As I told her the story, there was a tear in my mom's eyes. She said, "Mama was wearing that dress when she died."

Mama is my grandmother who was Papa's wife. "Looks like she was coming home to take him to heaven", she said.

To this day, every time I pass by the Johnson Funeral Home, I think about my grandmother coming to take my grandfather home to the heavens.

About the Author

Jennifer Carr lives in Santa Fe, New Mexico with her partner and two children. She is an EMT, journalist, writer, and poet. When she is not working at the local hospital or newspaper, she spends her time reading and writing. Her poetry and fiction have been published in print and online publications. Jennifer loves flying by her own wings and looks for any opportunity to soar to new heights.

Guardian Lycan

By Liam Pritchard

Convinced she is being pursued, Paige takes a detour, only to come face-to-face with a snarling werewolf. But is she the one who is really in danger?

He was still staring. Wobbling from side to side as the bus trundled through the failing twilight, Paige kept her head down, feigning interest in her phone but taking cursory glances at him in her peripheral vision and, sure enough, he was still staring.

From the second she'd stepped on the bus, his eyes had been on her. She'd briefly met his gaze as she walked up the gangway to the first available seat and the expression on his face turned her skin cold. He glared at her with an undisguised menace, forcing her to break the eye contact and look down at the floor.

She tried consoling herself that perhaps he wasn't looking that way specifically at her. Perhaps it was just bad timing and they both happened to look at each other at the same moment, and he was in possession of what her mum liked to call an "unfortunate face." But the way his whole body turned in his seat to face her as she passed and sat down herself dispelled that idea. He was staring directly at her and making no effort to at least pretend he wasn't.

She shuddered and glanced around at the other passengers in hopes of some sort of support but everyone had their heads either facing out the window or buried in their phone or a book. Everyone, that is, except him.

Unlocking her phone, she texted Danni.

"On the bus babe. Be about ten xx," she typed. After pressing send she added "there's some creep staring at me. It's freaking me out."

As she pressed send, the phone vibrated, and Danni's name flashed across the screen.

"K hun. Can't wait. Miss you xx."

And just as she was reaching the end of that, it buzzed again.

"Boo to the creep. Want me to come meet you? Xx"

She did. She really did, but she also didn't want Danni to think she was a silly little girl, who couldn't handle being looked at.

"No. It's ok," a thought crossed her mind. "He's probably autistic or something and doesn't realize it's rude to stare."

A sickening sensation of guilt swam through her stomach at this and she glanced up at him and flashed him a reassuring smile. Still he stared, his expression unchanged. Her eyes darted back to her phone.

They stayed there till it was her stop. The button pinged loudly in the silence as she pulled herself to her feet with the pole. She staggered forwards, struggling to maintain dignity in high heels as the vehicle rapidly decelerated. Keeping her eyes on the floor as she stumbled past him, she felt his eyes boring into her as his body shifted around to keep her in view.

Giving the driver a cursory "thank you" as the doors swung open, she flung herself down the steps and into the early evening gloom. As she powered away from the bus in the direction of home, she caught sight of a shape hopping off the bus as the doors snapped shut and headed in her direction.

Her stomach jumped into her throat as she craned her neck over her shoulder. It was him. His hands stuffed into his jacket pockets, eyes still fixed on her, he was striding after her.

For a moment she considered confronting him, after all, guys like this only pick on girls they think are weak, easy targets. But she could see he was a good foot taller than her and probably at least four stone heavier too. Like it or not, she was an easy target.

Quickening her pace, she fumbled for her phone.

"He's following me. I'm scared," her trembling fingers spelled out.

She took a crumb of comfort in the fact his speed had not increased with hers and she was beginning to put some extra distance between them. Maybe he wasn't following her after all. Maybe it really was his stop too and she was just being paranoid.

Regardless, she would rest easier without him on her tail so she took a slight detour, bearing left a hundred yards earlier than usual. After a few seconds of power walking, she checked over her shoulder to see that he hadn't yet emerged around the corner and took the next right to take her back on track without being spotted. For good measure, she took another left and then a right before heaving a sigh of relief.

She felt her phone buzz in her pocket as she stopped dead in her tracks. Up ahead, its yellow artificial light looming out of the darkness, was the underpass. Although it was only the width of four lanes of traffic and you could clearly see the other side, the place still gave her the creeps. She always avoided it, even in the daytime. She'd heard enough urban legends, and perhaps also true stories, of bad things happening to lone women who walked under such things.

Not a hope in hell, she thought.

Looking behind her again, she saw the coast was clear. He must have passed harmlessly on. It would be safe to back up a little and readjust course.

Heading back, she turned the corner and walked face-first into him, stumbling backward from the impact. Slightly disoriented, she saw him smiling at her. Not a kind smile, but a victorious one. A hungry one.

She screamed and ran toward the underpass, forgetting her reluctance from moments before. Despite her head start and her best efforts, his long strides devoured the ground between them. Echoes from her heels pounding the stone floor rang out as she went under the road and, as she looked ahead, she saw two other men appear in her path.

"Help me!" she shrieked at them, but any hope she might have had dissolved as they broke into a run towards her with the same hungry lust in their eyes.

Slowing her pace briefly as she tried to consider her options, heavy hands grabbed her from behind and spun her to face him. She swung a fist and connected with his temple. He staggered but held tight as she aimed a knee at his groin. He anticipated it, pivoting and taking the blow to his thigh. It hurt him, but not nearly enough.

His hand clasped her face, the fingertips pressing hard into her jaw bone and he dragged her face to his as his friends grabbed an arm each.

"If you're that desperate to touch it," he snarled, beginning to reach for his crotch. But his expression changed from rage to terror before he could finish his sentence.

Paige felt a sharp tug on her right arm, pulling her hard to the side before those hands let go. She saw the man from the bus running in the opposite direction as the man on her left also released her arm, leaving her to fall in a heap on the floor. A dark mass flashed over her and, in the blink of an eye, the man from the bus vanished, only the echo of a scream remained where he'd stood.

She rolled onto her back and saw the third man sprinting for the exit, whimpering like a small child. Before he could make it, a hulking black shape landed square on his back, forcing him face-down into the ground. In the same swift movement, it grabbed him by the scruff of his neck and lifted him clean off the ground and carried him, screaming, into the darkness.

Another scream rang out in the distance, followed by a crunch and then silence.

Lying on the floor, her heart pounding, a voice in Paige's head said "run."

Without thinking, she kicked off her heels, hauled herself to her feet, and made for the nearest exit as fast as she could. Not fast enough.

With a thud, the shape crashed to the floor mere feet in front of her, and she toppled onto her back.

The beast towered over her, lurching forwards on the knuckles of its long forearms. It had the form of a human, but its long arms reached all the way to the floor without stooping, and its body was entirely covered in thick black hair. Atop its gorilla-like torso was the shaggy head of a hound, blood

caked in a hairy muzzle that surrounded a row of razor-sharp teeth as long as her fingers.

She crawled backward, not taking her eyes off the creature as it padded slowly towards her. It had devoured the other three in quick, maybe not painless, deaths but clearly intended to savor her. Tears

pricked her eyelids as Danni sprang to mind and the realization she'd never see her again. She wished it would just kill her now and spare her that.

But the creature didn't attack. Its chest heaved from exertion and its shoulders drooped in a non-threatening stance. In its yellow eyes, she saw not aggression but compassion. It came closer, treading carefully and slowly. Its eyes begging and Paige felt her fear melt away.

Its face came closer to hers. She expected to smell rancid, hot breath, but there was instead a familiar sweetness and saliva formed on her tongue. Lifting a cautious hand, she stroked its head and it groaned contentedly.

A laugh escaped her lips and the creature made a noise that mirrored it, before nuzzling its forehead against hers. She stroked its fur with both hands and laughed some more.

Moments later, it withdrew and nudged her shoulder with its head, pointing her in the direction of the exit. She looked the way it was indicating, and when she turned back, she saw just its hind legs disappearing into the darkness. She was alone again.

She pulled herself to her feet and reached into her coat pocket for her phone.

"Hang tight. I'm on my way," read the earlier text from Danni.

Danni, Paige thought. She wouldn't know I came this way. How could she?

Panic began to rise in her chest just as Danni appeared in the archway. Paige ran to her, now sobbing. She tried to speak but only strangled noises came out.

Danni pulled her tight toward her, shushing her, stroking and kissing her hair. Her sweet perfume hit Paige's nose and as she looked up into her loving, yellow eyes, Danni whispered,

"You're safe now."

About the Author

Liam Pritchard is based in Wales in the UK. He began writing short horror fiction in 2016 after losing his job and self-publishing "The Girl with the Monkey on Her Shoulder" to modest success. A lean few years followed before a resurgence in 2019/2020 saw a number of his stories accepted for publication in various anthologies. He is presently studying screenwriting and plays tin whistle (badly) in a Pogues tribute band.

Lia's Tale
The Secret of the Rowan
By Patrick Tibbits

A bump along the path sent her seeking after light.

In that older time, before the woodland gnomes and water sprites were hidden from the eyes of folk, on a grey chilly spring morning with clumps of fog everywhere, as like to winter as spring, a young girl hurried along toward the village school.

Though she trod familiar flagstones, Lia fell, flat on her face. The smooth stones of the path had collected the morning mist, which had frozen clear and slippery as glass. She winced as a cold stone bit at the heels of her hands.

She lay for a moment as the shock faded. She pushed herself up, the cold of the ice stabbing her knees through her sturdy brown school dress. She searched for any who might have seen her pratfall. She was alone. Ahead, the close-laid stones of the path ran along a hedgerow where bushes crowded beneath thick old trees. A bare field, deep with early spring mud, lay along the other side. Its far border lay hidden in the grey chill mist. No bird called. No wind whispered. It was as though the mist had smothered all. Scents of leaf mold and wet earth were carried on the damp heavy air.

She had never stopped at this place before, always hurrying along to school, never ready quite early enough. The scene was made strange by man-sized grey whorls drifting slowly along just above the leaf litter of the hedgerow, out from the trees, across the path and into the field. She hugged herself against a chill. She took heart when she saw that the hedge here deepened into a grove of rowan trees, known to her folk as ancient wards against witchery.

Still stranger than the wisp-haunted air, a golden light glowed in the depths of the grove. The trunks of the rowan trees were straight black bars as if silhouetted by a warm yellow setting sun. It promised warmth and light on a mist-filled chilly wet day. She peered harder into the gloom beneath the trees. The glow lit the drifting wisps of mist as if from within. After a few moments, she lifted the strap of her book bag from her shoulder. Leaving it on the path, she crept into the grove, stepping carefully in soft wet leaves and fallen twigs. At odd times, droplets went *pupp* onto the leaf litter, fallen from the rowan branches. Else all was fog-soft silence.

She picked her way among wet bushes into the depths of the grove, wending toward where the light shone, losing sight of the path behind. Among the rowans, she feared no witchery but avoided the drifting grey wisps just the same. At length, she tiptoed around the bole of a large rowan tree and there, as if growing from the forest floor, were the head and torso of a small reddish-brown man. His arms were thin as a child's, and he twisted and pushed himself up through soft dark mud and sodden leaves until he worked himself free and stood, clothed only in streaks of black loam.

Lia steadied herself against the wet rough bark of the rowan as he turned his head to face her. He looked old. He had not a hair on his long narrow head. His low forehead wrinkled above a prominent nose, which curved down nearly to his pointed chin. His cheeks were lean and hollow, and deep furrows ran beside his nose and mouth. He turned his gaze to her, as though he saw perfectly well.

Yet his eyes were entirely grey, without white or pupil. She could feel his glance on the skin of her face.

"You've come, then," he said.

His voice was like midnight wind soughing through leafless trees, a sound that made her wakeful on winter nights. She looked into his empty gaze. She held silent because it was not in her mind to try to speak, so rapt was she with trying to understand what he was.

The little fellow turned from her and bent to inspect the leafy forest floor. He selected a single dead rowan leaf, fallen months before. He held it beneath his nose for a moment and then poked it into his mouth on the end of a long spindly index finger. He munched slowly, his head tilted a little to the side, as though he were considering the flavor. The must of wet leaves was strong.

The sunny glow shone up from a little chest, perhaps a jewel casket, which lay open near his feet. It lit the trunks of the rowans rich deep brown and turned the wisps to translucent sunset gold. The yellow brilliance in the chest was strong, too strong to see inside.

He bent to the chest, and the glow winked out as he closed the lid. The grove went dark, the rowans loomed up black. The cold grey clumps of mist drifted in the dimness.

"The light will be within then," he said.

The chest was no bigger than a rye loaf. It was of unfinished dark brown wood, with hinges and lock plate of brass dulled by wet and time. A small key, brass like the fittings but bright green with verdigris, rested in the lock.

He held the rounded lid shut, and twisted the key with a sharp snap. He withdrew the key and with a long index finger, pressed it to his lips. He *whooshed* in a long breath, and the key disappeared.

He said, "This is for you, then."

He held the chest out toward her and once again pressed his grey gaze upon her.

"What is it?" she asked.

"Your true desire. Your sorest need, then."

He stood unmoving, arms extended, grasping the chest between his palms. His index fingers were fully half again as long as the other fingers on each hand. They curled around onto the front of the chest. All the fingers were thin, crooked, and tapered to long points.

"You must take it then," he said.

She stepped forward and took the weight of the chest between her hands, one above and one below. It was as cold and wet as everything else within the grove and smelled of wet earth. She jumped as one of his fingers, rough as an old board, brushed against her hand.

He turned and strode, lifting his feet high, toward the burrow. His toes were much too long and thin and tapered to fine points like his fingers. The two big toes were longer still. He had to take care not to catch them in the wet leaves. He began wiggling feet first back into the muddy black earth.

"And who are you?" she asked.

"Remember me as Rowan, then."

He paused and looked back at her. His nose, too, tapered to a long thin sharp end. "Come to gather berries in the fall. You'd best go, then."

She was late to school that day. Else the day was like any other, save for her preoccupation. She every minute wondered what sort of elf or gnome she had met with, and puzzled over the little chest thrust down into her book bag. What might shine so in the chest, and why did she need it above all other things?

That evening, she put the chest on her shelf, in place of a stone she had used as a bookend. Lia was loved at home and little remarked at school, neither bright nor dull, pretty nor plain. She was a girl of the shire, brown-haired, hazel-eyed, who had seen eleven summers without causing great worry to her mother or the mistress at the school. The stories of the smallfolk had taught her what to do. She did not try the lid or lock and told no one of the chest. The smallfolk did not trifle, nor would she trifle with their gift. Given by a gnome, it was hers alone to keep.

Each following day was much like the days before she had met Rowan, except that she now came to wonder what she so desired and lacked. She supped each eve on good, plain fare and sheltered warm at night. If she had a need, it must be a lack within. Each morn as she left her room, and on return at eve, the sight of the little brown chest brought the puzzle back afresh.

In the fall of the year, just as the rowan leaves turned yellow, she returned to the grove and gathered red berries, each branded with its witch-ward, a pentagonal star. The berries grew in bunches, each on a thin stem. They were firm and only slightly sweet. From time beyond memory, they had been gathered by her folk when crops failed and famine stalked, but they were not much sought of late. Still, reverence clung to the trees.

She carried the little brown wooden chest in the berry bag slung across her chest. She searched for Rowan but found neither the little homunculus nor his burrow. The layer of dead leaves was unbroken. Prodding around with her walking staff found only soft black earth below the musty-smelling leaf mold. As she thrust deeper, her staff caught on the rowan roots, and they were reddish-brown and thin, yet hard to break.

Again she put the chest away. She asked her mother to show her how to make jam of the rowan berries, and her mother sent her to the drygoods shop to buy sugar.

Lia loved the dim little shop for its smells of tinned oils and sacks of grains, all stacked on sturdy wooden shelves. But on this visit, while she stood at the counter to give over her coppers for the packet of sugar, the quarrel happened.

The shopgirl said not a word to her, meeting Lia's eyes with a flat uncaring look. She was a little taller, a year or two older than Lia, a girl with the light curls and eyes of the folk from the western shires. On the point of greeting her, Lia instead returned the look, her face too without expression, and she said nothing. Her nerves wound tight as she pushed the coppers across the counter. The shopgirl counted Lia's copper coins, and once more gazed without expression at her. Lia's arms were stiff as she picked up the sugar and turned to go. The two young women had said nothing at all, but each felt the wound of their silent quarrel.

Another young woman, almost any other young woman, would have thought the clerk terribly rude. And Lia did think her terribly rude. Yet it occurred to her, as had become her unconscious habit, to think on what might be needful. Perhaps the chest held a charm, something that would ease the tension of the quarrel. She went to her bookshelf, but the chest remained tightly closed.

Over the next few days, the quarrel came to her in odd moments. Her mind worried at it and her belly felt unwell and she wished to be free of it. What had she been lacking? She saw herself, mirroring the shopgirl's uncaring stare, and she knew somehow that what was important was not the shopgirl's coldness, but her own. She saw then what was needful.

It was nearly a fortnight later that her mother sent Lia to the shop again. Lia thought of the shopgirl on her way to the market, and as she gathered tea and flour from the shelves. As she walked toward the counters at the front of the shop, Lia saw that the same girl stood at one counter. The other was attended by a slender boy with flame-red hair. There was something interesting about the young man, but Lia paused and then walked to the young woman's counter.

The girl saw Lia approaching, and her face fell. She gave a little shake to her head. It was plain that she expected a renewal of their quarrel. Lia set her items on the counter and met the young woman's flat gaze. Though her belly chilled with fright, she said, "I'm sorry I was rude the other day."

The girl froze, her gaze locked on Lia. Then her jaw dropped and her eyes popped wide as she realized what Lia had said. For just that instant she and the girl stood in a wash of brilliant golden light. The counter girl held Lia's eyes, looking overwhelmed. A great current of feeling coursed through Lia, and she thought she must look very much the same. The two of them stared in silent recognition. Moments passed before the shopgirl said, "Oh, that's alright."

Lia looked around the shop but saw that the only light came from the front windows, and was dim and silvery. She thought that something like an explosion must have happened, but the shopboy at the next counter and the women looking at shelves of sundries appeared to have noticed nothing.

She looked back to the counter and put down her coppers. The shopgirl counted them. She looked at Lia again. Still a little stunned, they nodded to one another.

As Lia made her way back home, she thought of what she had seen in the shopgirl's face, how it had been already within her, a part of her, and how she had found something very like it within herself. The light that had lit the cold mist in the rowan grove had for an instant flashed upon them. And she thought that having Rowan's little brown wooden chest had shown her a thing to be much desired.

Each autumn, she returned to the grove but found there only berries. She came to know the counter clerks in the drygoods shop. To everyone she knew, she offered jars of russet jam. They wondered at her kindness, but few wanted such plain preserves.

Lia never saw the golden light again, though she lived her life in seeking. When a thing went wrong or she argued with her mother or quarreled with a friend, she gave herself to thought, her meditation fixed on what it was she most desired, and on what was needful in her. When she came to know the remedy, then she acted, though that part was never easy. Every now and then, Lia looked into a set of eyes and shared in joy.

At her wedding, her bridesmaid was a young woman from the western shires, fair of eye and hair. After, the chest went onto another shelf, one in her pantry, up high. Children grew and departed. Her husband, a slender fellow with auburn hair, and her children thought she looked at them a little oddly sometimes.

She began to be a little bent and went white at her crown. Jars of rowanberry jam lined the shelf alongside the little chest.

There came a day when she shuffled along the flagstone path, thinking she would not see another fall. Yet she felt clear as rainwater when she saw the sumac afire with crimson leaves and berries, and the rowans with their bright yellow leaves, and heavy with their own red berries.

Her every step into the wood crunched newly fallen leaves. She paused near the center of the grove. There was a rustling and sure enough, she stepped around a great trunk to spy Rowan struggling to birth himself once again from the black loam.

The little red-brown man wriggled his torso free of the earth. He was as she remembered, all thin limbs and pointy nose. He pushed himself up and took two strides away from the burrow, careful to lift his feet with their long splayed toes. He plucked a fresh-fallen leaf from a yellow heap of them and crushed it in his thin bent fingers beneath his nose. He nodded, and let the powder fall.

"The grove is well then," he said. The words were a whisper of wind.

He reached out his twisty brown arms, and she placed the chest in his hands. Clasping it in his long thin fingers, he set it on the forest floor.

Rowan coughed, like a gust from an autumn storm. He coughed a dozen times more before he reached to his lips for the little brass key he had hidden a lifetime ago.

"I have no need to see," said Lia.

Rowan turned his blank grey eyes to her. He smiled, his thin lips pulling back along his long head.

"Nor have I. You have come to stay, then."

He fitted the key to its lock but left it unturned. He took up the little chest and turned toward his burrow.

Lia lay back in the cushion of dry leaves, their dusty spice rising about her. She closed her eyes. She would rest forever here among the rowans, ancient friends of the folk. High above her, the setting sun shone through their bright yellow crowns, and the grove was filled with pure golden light.

About the Author

Patrick Tibbits is a survivor, so far, of a 1960s adolescence, an atypical neurological organization, and graduate study in engineering and applied mathematics. He has three college degrees and discharge certificates from two additional institutions.

The Day the River Freezes
By C. Marry Hultman

An old army buddy recalls the Urban Legend of the deadly River Lady.

This was told to me by my grandfather who had heard it from an old army buddy during a card game at the VA Hall. It had come up as the old gentlemen discussed near brushes with death. My grandfather's friend, whom he had known since their Case High School days and had been a prominent member of the city government asserted that he was lucky to be alive after his encounter with the Woman of Washington Park. Naturally, the other veterans around the card table were intrigued and since their friend was a storyteller of some note, they implored him to recount his tale.

****

It was some time after the war and my grandfather's acquaintance had found himself a job working as an usher at The Capitol, an old movie theatre in West Racine. As such, he was always the last one to lock up for the evening, long after everyone else had gone home for the night. On this particular occasion, it was in the middle of one of those frigid winters one only gets in the Midwest. Complete white-out blizzards, temperatures so low that old folks freeze to death, you know the kind.

He had just locked up for the evening when he noticed that, the otherwise clear, cold night, had turned hazy and gray. In fact, the snow was coming down with such intensity that he could barely see more than a couple of feet in front of him. Since he was without a vehicle at the time and it was far too late and inclement to find a cab, he decided to attempt walking home through the woods surrounding Washington Park and follow the Root River. It was something he did most nights anyway so he was familiar with the route. The difference was that there was zero visibility, and he had to be extra careful not to wander into the river by mistake.

As he took the first tentative steps across the snow-covered street, he heard the sound for the first time. He said it sounded like someone or something singing far off in the distance. It was difficult to make out clearly due to the harsh wind muffling it, but to him, it sounded like a solitary lamentation, like a melody somewhat familiar. He convinced himself that it was just a trick of nature and began his trek home through the now ankle-deep snow. Some days, when the sky was clear and the wind less oppressive he might stroll on more unbeaten paths, but this night he found it wisest to take a more familiar trail, wider and with the river to his right. A more direct route towards Oak Street and the boarding house where he lived.

He tried to huddle up against the frigid gales desiring to cause him frostbite, while still being mindful of where he tread when he once again heard the distant tones of a person singing on the wind. This time it was louder and more distinct. It sounded sorrowful. Very much like emotional pain expressed in music. It pulled at his heartstrings causing him to feel a need to investigate. He looked around to see if he could locate the origin of the chorus, but there was only the white snow covering the ground and the branches surrounding him. He could see his tracks quickly covered up; almost trying to hide that he had ever walked there. This time the sound did not cease. He noticed as he climbed the steep hill, trying not to slide backward, to meet up with the river on the other side that the voice grew in intensity. As it did so, it started tugging at him. He could not quite explain it. It was as if the melody had formed some sort of disembodied hand, enveloping him and pulling him closer. He attempted to stand still, but his legs pushed on, ignoring his command. Now, my grandfather's friend was unsure of what was going on. It felt as if the sound was clear, yet his ears were cold and sensitive so he believed it might well have been an illusion. A trick of nature, caused by the darkness, weather, and the desolate woods around him.

As he descended the hill, he realized that the river must have frozen over completely, because he could no longer tell where it flowed. Through the haze of icy precipitation, he could barely make out a wide-open area lined by tall trees where the river must surely be. It would be equally difficult to discern where it began and ended. How far from the trees could he venture before he risked falling through the ice?

Just before the Sixth Street Bridge and with the eerie sound of the melody intensifying, he noticed a shape off in the distance. Not on the narrow path he was on, but off to the side in the open area among the trees. He slowed down and tried to get a clear view of what it was through the curtain of snow. At first, he was convinced it must be some kind of animal. One that does not hibernate in winter, so maybe a dog or cat, but as the song beckoned him closer, he thought it looked like a person, perhaps kneeling in the snow. Suddenly insight struck him as if his brain had just derived a conclusion. The song was coming from this creature.

His feet continued moving on their own as the melody still drew him in. Once he realized what he was doing, he called out to the shape. The singing did not cease, but it looked like the person turned towards him. He moved closer still, the snow died down and the wind became no more than a whisper on his skin. He noticed that it was a girl, a teenager maybe, clad in a white dress and with thick red hair cascading in front of her face. Maybe she had been stuck in the snow for some time, for there were no tracks around her still frame. She might also be injured, he assumed, for there did not seem to be any reason for her to stay put if she could move. Was she the victim of some accident? Maybe she had hurt herself walking home. Had she broken through the ice, and only appeared to be kneeling?

He tried to halt his progress, but the voice called to him with such beautiful power that he could not stop. Now that the wind had died down and his vision was unobstructed, the song was so much brighter. It reminded him of his mother singing him to sleep, of a choir in church or carolers on a Christmas morning. He wanted to find his bearing before he continued. To be level headed so that he could offer her the proper assistance, but something was obstructing his actions. He felt it pulling at him, an icy grip encouraging him to move on. As he took struggling steps towards her, she stretched out her arms at him, and he felt compelled to be close to her, not so much to save her, more like being with her. The singing continued and in the cold night air, all he could think of was how warm her embrace would be. His mind was hazy and he knew deep down inside that he was not thinking straight, why would he otherwise be moving with such ease into a situation he knew nothing about?

Something told him that he should not, yet every fabric of his being wanted to wrap himself around her and hear that sweet voice softly sing into his ear. To lull him to sleep like a babe nestled in her arms. The scent of lavender filled his nostrils. It was the smell of his mother's house after she had cleaned his room. Memories of snuggling down between clean sheets and then waking up to a hearty breakfast. The heavy aroma of bacon had replaced the lavender, and then home-baked chocolate chip cookies. It was as if his senses were being flooded by happy recollections of a time long gone. Before he went to war and saw what men could do to one another.

Although her face was still behind the tangle of red hair, her form mesmerized him. Her dress was far from modern. It instead reminded him of something his grandmother would have worn. Something he had seen in an old photograph. Too fancy to be something to wear on an everyday occasion. He stretched out his arms to meet hers. Those milky white arms with yellowed, broken fingernails, like claws. The sight of them caught him off guard, brought him back.

Then, as if by chance, his gaze fell down where she sat and noticed something even stranger, something he had not paid attention to before. The woman was not stuck in the snow at all and she was not kneeling either. She was floating, ever so slightly above the ground, the snow and her billowing dress creating the illusion. As he noticed the startling fact, he heard the ice crack below his feet. He had walked out on to the river without noticing it. He backed off, suddenly free from whatever hex had enchanted him, and the girl stopped her singing. He looked up from his feet and saw a horrific sight. The girl's red hair had fallen away from her face to reveal rotting skin pulled tightly over a skull-like form. Black eyes stared at him and a mouth of putrid teeth. He cried out and backed away when the thing screamed and grabbed at him. He dodged the boney fingers and fell over. A dull echo reverberated across the landscape as he hit the ice and he was certain he felt it break. The creature unfolded from its position and began crawling towards him, snarling as she grabbed at his legs. Now that the spell was broken the snow, but instead of singing, the woman emitted a shrill scream that blended with the howling wind. He created space by crawling backward from her and then rolled over to his stomach. Her hands clasp his right leg and he howled in pain as her fingernails dug into his calf. He wriggled free and with blood leaving a trail in the snow he ran. Ran without looking back. Only hearing the screeching slowly drowning in the blizzard.

    Once back at the boarding house the woman who ran the establishment set him by the fireplace and gave him a brandy. She told him she had been worried sick about him. Every time there was a blizzard of this kind, she said, someone always seemed to walk through the ice of the river. Maybe because they believed it to be frozen solid and wanted to take a shortcut home. She had come to expect the authorities to fish out a corpse after every such storm. She assured him he was very lucky that he avoided being another victim of the treacherous river running through the woods.

****

That might have been the end of the tale. It was at least the end of his part. When my grandfather's acquaintance had finished recounting his experience another vet, who had been sitting at an adjoining table, leaned over.

He claimed to have heard of the woman in the woods of Washington Park. Some of the tales told to him were second-hand accounts and some were from those who had espied the specter from a distance. It was always the same story though. Always a snowstorm. A young woman singing a melancholy melody beckoning wanderers to come to her sitting on the frozen river in the center of the woods, trying to lure people out on the fragile ice.

Another old man chimed in after having heard this and told them that his brother had experienced the mysterious woman too. He had broken through the ice and the cold from the river had broken the trance. Luckily, he had managed to pull himself out from the icy water and had avoided the creature's grasp.

After his experience, the brother had ventured to the public museum to see if he could find out anything more about this mysterious woman since she appeared to be infamous in the area around Washington Park. In an old book about the history of the city, he found an article that, according to the brother, made his blood run cold as if he was still in that icy water. Attached was a black-and-white photograph of a young woman clad in a fancy white dress. The article read that her body the authorities pulled out of the river in 1840. That winter there had been a terrible blizzard and the City's first bridge crossing had frozen stiff, causing it to collapse and fall into the river below. The only casualty had been a young, red-haired woman, who was waiting for her fiancé to take her away to Chicago so they could marry according to the newspaper article he found she was a singer and was hoping to find work in the music halls of The Windy City. The picture was of the woman who had tried to lure him in the woods in the blizzard.

I never walk through the Washington Park Woods alone anymore.

About the Author

C. Marry Hultman is a teacher, writer, and sometimes podcaster who is equal parts Swede and Wisconsinite. He lives with his wife and two daughters and runs W.A.R.G. – THE Guild podcast dedicated to interviewing authors about their creative process. In addition to that, he runs the website Wisconsin Noir – Cosmic Horror set in the Dairy State, where he collects short fiction and general thoughts.

Find out more about him on Twitter @stoughe, on Facebook @WisconsinNoir, and at the following website: https://wisconsinnoir.wixsite.com/wisnoir

Silent Moments
By Kimberly Gray

Katelyn Mitchell had a crush on her childhood friend, and when her brother brings him to a meeting, she realizes she still does. Trying to establish a ghost-hunting team is hard enough without the added distraction. As she debates whether or not to tell him, he surprises her with a confession of his own.

Katelyn Mitchell looked around her living room. Her brother was always late. *He'd better have a good excuse this time.* She opened her mouth to get the meeting started, but her brother Noah burst through the door. And he wasn't alone. Katelyn swallowed hard.

"I know. I know. I'm late. But, Adrian just moved back, and we've been hanging out and catching up. I told him what we're doing, and he wants to come along. Is that okay?"

Katelyn hadn't realized she was staring at Adrian until her brother snapped his fingers in her face. He looked so different, yet still the same.

"That's alright, isn't it?" Her brother asked again.

"Yes. That's fine. We'll all have to get together later. But, right now, we need to go over where we're going."

Katelyn's best friend Emma Landry and her boyfriend Gavin Shaffer set at the ready for notes. She loved their eagerness.

"Alright. We've all heard the tales that supposedly go on in Pleasant View Cemetery. Tonight, we are going there to see if we can catch anything on film. Now, this cemetery is no longer in use, so be careful where you go. The dates may be faded, but we should be able to go to the archives for all that. So, who's ready?"

They all stood up and made a beeline for the door. When Adrian passed Katelyn, he smiled. Her heart fluttered. She guessed her foolish childhood crush on him was still around. Katelyn would dare not tell him back then and probably wouldn't now. While the others talked, She remained silent. She hoped she could keep her focus and not do anything stupid. They pulled up to the cemetery entrance.

"This place is creepy at night," Noah said.

"It's creepy in the day time," Emma reminded him.

"Everyone got their gear? Keep your flashlights and walkies on. We can all go together, or we can go off in different directions."

"Gavin and I will go together."

"I'd prefer you take someone else with you."

Noah spoke up. "I'll go with them."

Katelyn shot him a glare. He smiled.

"Let's head out. Meet back here at 2 o'clock."

The trio walked one way, and Katelyn and Adrian started another way.

"I'm glad I'm going with you. It's been so long since we saw each other. You've grown up."

"What is that supposed to mean?" Katelyn snapped, not meaning to.

"Nothing. Just you've matured. You're a woman now. You were still a kid the last time I saw you. It's just strange in a way, you know. It was strange seeing Noah grown up. All my memories are kids."

Katelyn stopped him from going on.

"I get it. You look different, too. Not how I pictured you to look, though."

"But, you did picture me?"

"Many times," she said as she stared off into space.

So, do I look better or worse than you imagined?"

"Better," Katelyn all but sighed.

She shook her head. They were there to hunt ghosts. Not take a trip down memory lane.

"Do you want to do an EVP session?"

"Sure."

Katelyn turned the voice recorder on and set it down.

"I've thought about you, too."

Katelyn put her finger up to her mouth.

"Sorry," Adrian whispered.

"Is there anyone here?"

She waited before asking another question.

"Is there something you need or want to say?"

Again, she paused. Adrian placed his hand over hers. She knew it had to be his hand because it came from his direction, otherwise she'd be scared. Katelyn shined her flashlight toward his face, and he smiled. She smiled back. It seemed he was trying to tell her something but couldn't because they were recording.

"Let's go further into the cemetery and try again."

She stopped the recorder, and they proceeded. The moon peeked out from behind a cloud making the atmosphere spookier than it already was.

"What have you been doing with yourself?" Adrian asked.

"I'm taking nursing in college. I want to be a labor and delivery nurse."

"That's awesome. I'm taking law enforcement."

"A cop, huh? That's cool."

"You don't sound impressed."

"It's not that. I just didn't see you as a cop. I guess we've all changed so much. Just be careful when you get out there."

"I will."

Before they walked any further, Adrian grabbed Katelyn's arm.

"Look. I have to tell you. I liked you when we were kids. And upon seeing you again, I still do. I wanted to get that out there."

Katelyn felt her cheeks burn. He liked her, too. She told herself she wouldn't tell him, but he put himself out on a limb. She might as well do it, too.

"I liked you, too. And I still do. I have thought about you quite a lot."

"So, do you want to go out? Be my girlfriend and all that?"

Katelyn giggled. "Sure."

Adrian came closer and bent his head down. He cupped her face with both hands. Katelyn looked into his eyes. A little bit more, and she'd be hyperventilating. Her crush was about to kiss her. At least, she hoped he was. And when his lips came down on hers in a gentle embrace, she almost melted. Some people would think it was weird, kissing in a cemetery. But, Katelyn forgot where they even were. Adrian broke the kiss.

"We need to be getting back, don't we?"

Katelyn looked at her watch.

"Oh goodness. I can't believe it's so late. Time sure has flown by. Let's go."

They made their way back to the entrance. As they were coming up on it, they met Noah, Emma, and Gavin.

"Any luck?" Katelyn asked.

"No. We did a few EVP sessions but nothing visual happened."

"We did one, too."

Noah looked up and started stammering, "G-Guys. Is that a person?"

They all looked where he was pointing. A man who appeared to be glowing was limping by the gate. They could make out that he was an elderly man with a white beard. He wore nautical clothing like a sea captain with a matching cap.

Katelyn whispered, "Everyone, get your cameras out. Take pics and videos."

They did that for a bit before Katelyn yelled, "Hey! Hey Mister!"

And with that, the man faded before their eyes. They all glanced at one another with wide eyes and mouths agape.

"Please tell me we got that," Katelyn said, still a bit shaken.

Everyone played their videos and looked through their pictures.

"Yes, we did."

"This is…awesome!" Katelyn jumped for joy.

They left for Katelyn's house, where they reviewed their EVP recordings. They were bummed they didn't catch anything on them, but the video evidence of the man was enough to prove that Pleasant View Cemetery was haunted.

"Alright, everyone. So, do we want to go to other places and do this again?"

"Yes!" They all shouted in unison.

"We can make our own online channel showing us on our ghost hunts. What about that?"

"Cool!" Again, everyone agreed.

"Now, we need a name."

Emma came up with an idea first.

"What about Beyond The Grave Trackers?"

Katelyn thought for a bit.

"I like it."

The room filled with "Yeahs" and "Cools" as the others voiced their agreements.

"So, that will be what our channel will be called. Oh, and me and Adrian are together."

Everyone grew quiet. Noah walked up to Adrian and slapped him on his back.

"It's about time! Man, I've been knowing the two of you liked each other since childhood. But, we need to leave. I'm tired. Come on, Adrian. See you guys tomorrow."

"Bye."

Adrian kissed Katelyn, and the others broke into "Oohs".

"Come on, guys. What are we? Kids still?"

Gavin and Emma left, leaving Katelyn by herself. She thought about the events of the night. And all in all, it turned out to be wonderful. She would have to forgive

Noah for being late this time since it led to her and Adrian getting together. Before she closed her eyes, she smiled, feeling happier than she had in some time.

The End

About the Author

When not writing, Kim spends time with her two kids and her husband in Northwest Alabama. She enjoys listening to music, reading, crocheting, watching television, and completing word search puzzles. She has always had a love of reading, which grew into a love for writing. She's a big Alabama football fan and loves the Dallas Stars hockey team.

I Could Not Stop for Death

By Katelyn Cameron

Moving into a new home is stressful, especially when your roommate died centuries ago. A woman goes on a quest to resolve her new haunted house and finds unexpected love among the answers.

The house was tall for standing at three stories, looming over the newer ranch-style homes and two-stories around it who had chosen efficiency over grandeur. Generations, decades, now centuries of history poured over the Massachusetts neighborhood, eroding memories as houses were demolished and rebuilt. This one stood above it all; it watched the ages unconcerned by the changes in fashion. It wore the 19th century like a lapel pin, given as a longevity award for surviving countless urban renewals and attempts to pave the future over the past.

Melanie hadn't gotten around to really learning her house yet. The furniture was moved in and organized, the pantry was stocked, but the things about a house, their loose floorboards and sticking doors were still foreign to her.

Her sense of modernity clashed horribly with the house's antiquated prestige. A large television rested flush against one wall and even her old-styled dining room set was too perfect to have been truly made by hand. A home like this should belong to a family, but Mel was alone. Her father insisted she live there when he opted to live in a retirement community and so it was that a home for a family from before the Civil War was the bachelorette pad of a twentysomething in the 21st century. The juxtaposition of classic and contemporary was at first unsettling but it grew on her. It felt like a poem composed by an interior decorator.

She set her book down and looked around the living room. It felt cold. Then again, it always felt cold. She wanted a life somewhere where winter was a theoretical construct and not an actual season. Obligation more than anything brought her into the cold land of Massachusetts. Maybe she needed to stoke her fireplace.

She set the book down and rose to light a nice flame when the whistle of a tea kettle caught her attention. Tea would be a lovely way to drive back the nearing winter season. She did have a kettle on the stove but had forgotten turning it on to boil. What tea to use it in remained an unresolved question in her life. She approached the kettle on her stovetop and the curiosity of forgetting she had set it to boil became a point of genuine concern.

She hadn't turned the stove on at all. The dial rested firmly on the "off" position. And yet the kettle whistled and spilled a stream of steam into the cold air.

Her blue eyes went wide and distant.

Thoughts raced through her mind: the kettle wasn't electric, the stove could be broken, the dangerousness of a broken stove, the cold, the chance that she was dreaming, the chance that she was losing her mind – she was under so much stress after all. Schizophrenia can manifest in someone's twenties, she had heard. Was she insane? Do insane people ask that question?

And the whistle of the kettle cut through those thoughts with its crisp improbability.

And Mel walked away. She had to walk away. There wasn't anything else she could do. Stand in the kitchen and lose her marbles? That wasn't a very good option. If she walked away, the kettle would stop eventually.

Hopefully. Besides, she clearly needed sleep. That was a sleep deprivation hallucination, it had to be.

By week's end, she had all but forgotten the tea kettle incident. She had a new job as a paralegal for a small and friendly law firm in Amherst. There was a lot of work to do. Not a lot of time to think about a slow descent into madness. She was thankful that she was able to keep busy, though admittedly would have been more thankful with another dollar an hour or so. Worry, too, was a welcome distraction.

She'd considered talking to friends about what happened, or how she was feeling in general, but since it sounded crazy when she thought about it she didn't dare express those thoughts aloud. And, most of the time, she was able to forget it ever happened.

The kettle incident came to mind albeit briefly as she washed her hair after a long day's work before a cozy weekend at home. Probably the association of hot water and boiling kettles. But singing a few bars of a catchy song playing on her cell phone pushed the memory aside again.

A song and a hair rinse later her phone chirped off. She had half her battery still when she got into the shower, had she really been in there that long? Probably, the water wasn't exactly warm anymore. The relaxation had been nice at least. So, with a heavy heart, Mel turned off the water and pulled her towel down from where she had thrown it over the shower's curtain.

She dried herself quickly, letting her wet dark brown hair frame her without worrying too much about taking a hairdryer to it, and went to pick her phone up from its place in the sink – it acted as a great boost for the phone's speaker. She thought back to the kettle again as she read the words written in the steam on her mirror.

"Welcome home".

Brian put a forkful of waffle in his mouth the following, an action he judged as better than glancing at Mel humorlessly. He chased that down with a sip of his water and finally gave his friend a stern, sober glance. "Welcome home."

"That's what it said," explained Mel. Brian, her closest friend, at least in terms of geography, was her confidant over Belgian waffles and a very strong cup of coffee. Tea had lost its appeal.

They sat in a local restaurant. She had called him first thing in the morning and he had answered the call because he found her rather attractive and she said she needed help. He hadn't expected to hear ghost stories.

"Well," he took a slow, steady breath to buy himself time to choose his words, "either your house missed you while you were at work or you need to call the police."

"No one came into the bathroom while I was in the shower," she said adamantly.

He nodded and wore the look of begrudgingly explaining something to a child. "Rubbing alcohol or shaving cream can prevent mirrors from misting up after a steamy shower. You have a stalker, Melanie."

He interrupted her before she could protest: "What's the alternative? You're haunted?"

Maybe she just preferred a supernatural threat to a real one, but she found herself fixated again on the tea kettle.

There was nothing abnormal about the kettle itself, and she was sure she'd have seen someone turn the burner off if it was a human being instead of some specter.

But she didn't mention the kettle. She wasn't entirely sure why she didn't mention it, but she didn't. "Well," she said instead, "I'll report it today."

She intended to. She really did. It was the responsible thing to do and it made so much more sense that the invader was flesh and blood. But instead of going to the police she just drove around Amherst. Each time she resolved to head to the police station she would turn away, afraid of confronting the possible reality Brian had mentioned. Eventually, when she just couldn't keep circling the town, she returned home.

Home was beginning to be a place of discomfort after the message in the mirror and the morning's discussion about it, so Mel decided it needed to be fortified. She made sure the windows were closed and that nothing was notably out of sorts. When she was satisfied nothing was amiss she went to her bedroom. A nap would help her relax, and she needed that right now.

She was watching the slow spin of a ceiling fan as her mind turned over the possibilities. Why was it that the idea of being haunted sat better with her than the idea of being stalked? A stalker was a threat she could face, one she could deal with. Then again, ghosts weren't real. The imagined was so much safer than the real.

A shiver ran through her. Not the cold shiver of fear or the kind that tries to bring heat to a body in need of it, but a shiver different altogether. A gentle shiver ran through

Mel. It felt pleasing, even intimate. Why would she have such a sensation now? It only lasted a few seconds and shortly after it faded the fan ceased to spin.

What made the fan stop? Just another unlikely thing in a week of unlikely things, she told herself. And she drifted quietly to sleep.

"Professional medium and paranormal advisor Lady Katla," Mel read aloud to herself and frowned at her laptop screen. "Consulting services available at reasonable rates."

It sounded so ridiculous. Then again, she was convinced she was being haunted. It was time to reevaluate what was realistic. If ghosts were real it would mean that the people who claimed to interact with them weren't automatically charlatans. Maybe Lady Katla was legit? She did have many positive reviews.

Katrina Laila Rosen, better known in the paranormal hobbyist circles as Katla, was beautiful. Sky-blue eyes, flawless skin, wheat-blonde hair, and a bit of extra height made her memorable. She dressed corporate casual and wore her wavy hair down. There were hints of a Swedish accent that seemed pushed to a greater-than-normal intensity to give her more 'eccentricity'. She carried a doctor's bag filled with tools of the paranormal trade and wore a long coat and a scarf fighting back the crisp New England fall.

"Good afternoon, Miss Loring," Katla bowed to Mel, setting her medical bag on a small table by the door. She offered a gloved hand to the other woman so politely and curiously that it immediately defined her as charming.

And this dashing investigator did catch Mel off-guard. She took Katla's hand and shook it. She hadn't expected her ghost hunter to be so elegant. Self-assured, certainly, but Katla was more than that. Cool confidence radiated from her and it made Mel feel so much calmer.

"I imagine you feel like you're going crazy," Katla said, opening her bag and producing several impressive pieces of equipment. She turned a pair of small cameras on and handed them to Mel as she fetched some other equipment. "But you shouldn't be. The supernatural world is very real, and I face it every day."

Of course it was, and of course she did. If Mel wasn't living this insanity she would have thought the blonde needed serious medications. But this was her life. So something about the pure conviction Katla spoke with that would've caused Mel to roll her eyes otherwise was a great comfort now.

After turning on an overly-expensive machine meant to read electromagnetic frequencies in the air, Katla pulled out a small bag of sage and a lighter. That seemed slightly out of place with the high technology approach, but Mel accepted it.

"Burning sage makes the home less hospitable to the spirit," explained Katla with the same clarity of purpose. "It will help us drive him out once we find him. Is there a bowl or something that I can put this in?"

"Y-yeah," nodded Mel. She was just blown away by the paranormal consultant's professionalism and confidence. Katla seemed to know everything and have an answer before a question even was asked. Even her voice, her posture, her wavy hair, and glittering eyes, it all gave her a sense of calm she hadn't had all week.

Mel led Katla to the dining room where the burning sage leaves were dropped into an empty fruit bowl. Katla proceeded to take the cameras from Mel and place one in the kitchen and the other in the bathroom. Those were where activity had been, after all. Then, she went back to her bag and produced a tablet computer.

Displayed on the screen were the kitchen and bathroom in shades of blue, green, and orange. Infrared or thermal imaging or something, Mel assumed. She had seen television monster chasers before and recognized some of Katla's tools. Of course, the people on television didn't look like Katla.

"The Cross compels you," Katla began. "The Star and Crescent compel you. The Wheel of Dharma compels you. The Star of David compels you." She handed the EMF to Mel and began to walk around the house, naming holy symbols and eventually repeating the list.

After making their way back to the burning sage in the dining room Katla's list of symbols ended, replaced by a very firm, commanding tone. "Dark spirit, you do not belong here. I command you to return home. Go back whence you came." She reached into the pocket of her coat and produced a stone and a hunk of wood, both roughly the size of a small coin.

It was a very mystic little ritual and seemed so informed and was performed so confidently it really seemed like something that would work.

Katla dropped the wood into the fire. She held the stone, a black gemstone, over the bowl of burning leaves and wood. "We ask you, please leave this space." And she also dropped the gemstone in the bowl.

The two stood silently as the sage and wood burned in the fruit bowl.

After a moment in the stillness, Mel finally started asking questions. "What are we burning?"

Katla responded quickly as if she had known the question would come eventually. "I start with sage that I grow myself and have blessed by holy men and add Palo Santo, a sacred wood from the Amazon rainforest. Lastly, we use a black tourmaline. Sage is an irritant to spirits and the holy energy from the wood enhances the flame, letting us burn the cleansing power into the stone. It's very old hedge magic I learned from particularly skilled magi in Prague."

It was such an impressive answer. Skilled magi and holy wood and black tourmaline all sounded very important and on the same level that being haunted made sense Mel figured that answer made sense too.

"Well," she hesitated. She wasn't sure she wanted to know the answer to her other question but asked it anyway. Nothing ventured, nothing gained. "Why me?"

Katla shrugged but again went into an answer as if she knew the question too well. "Spirits have any number of reasons for haunting the living. Maybe he was traumatized and can't move on, or maybe he has a connection to this place deeper than we can understand. Maybe he's in love with you, or he gave in to his darkness in life and fears judgment."

All traces of orange and yellow faded from one of the feeds on Katla's tablet but she didn't seem to notice. Instead, she kept talking.

"The important part is that we've asked him to leave. And once the sage and holy wood burns down you'll have a gemstone to keep your home spirit-free," explained the expert. "It's your ward against the hostile spirit."

Mel was profoundly thankful. The smoke rising out of the fruit bowl relaxed her, and she was sure that it repelled the spirit that was troubling her. 'Spirit' seemed to be the word Katla liked to refer to the ghost so Mel opted to defer to her expert on that subject.

The small fire in the fruit bowl continued to burn down.

Katla caught Mel's glance and smirked at her client. "By the way, I noticed." She turned her eyes back to the burning concoction in the bowl.

Mel scrunched up her face. "Noticed?" That was an odd thing to say. "Noticed what?" She wasn't sure what might've been noticed. Maybe the coldness on the tablet?

"The way you look at me."

Oh, that's what she noticed.

"I apologize," Mel was flustered and blushing at the observation. "I didn't mean… you just were…"

"If you want to get dinner sometime, I know a nice place," she didn't look up from the burning sage. She was too cool for that.

Mel was struck, silent. The woman who came to her rescue wanted to take her on a date? She was actually being hit on by another woman? She wasn't used to being hit on by people she wanted to be hit on by. It was a delightful sensation. She felt validated, warm, and like for once, the world was actually catering to her needs.

Katla led Mel back to her bag of equipment after gathering up her cameras and her EMF machine and produced an invoice. "Now, for the investigation and elimination of the spirit there's a service charge of two hundred plus expenses," she handed the slip of paper to her client. "I'll pick you up Thursday night?"

"Uh," Mel swiped a credit card on the investigator's tablet, "that sounds nice, yeah."

And for a while things were quiet. The dinner on Thursday went magnificently – Katla did know a delightful little place and she paid for their meal. She even offered to place other protective magics on Mel's house at a special discounted rate. It was all a lot for Mel to take in, but she nodded anyway and asked if she could learn more about the supernatural world from Katla. At reasonable rates, naturally.

Mel found herself lying on her couch a week or so after the cleansing ritual, playing with the little stone she had been given to ward away her unwanted guest. Katla made her more comfortable. She was a little suspicious about the sorceress' motivations, truly. She wasn't so oblivious as to not notice that work came up at dinner. Still, she was confident there was honestly a connection between them.

Something special. After all, Katla had saved Mel, which earned her the benefit of the doubt, right?

She slowly shifted to a sitting position and grabbed the remote. It didn't do her much good doubting herself, she wasn't about to change her mind about things. So she started streaming a movie to help her calm down. Something light and fun sounded right after the time she had lately.

A little laughter and a lot of letting her guard down later and the credits rolled. She decided to get up and get a drink but found herself unable. As she struggled against the unseen force, pressure began to pool on her lap to prevent her from rising.

Not again. No, it couldn't be!

The television's image went fuzzy and it clicked off.

She clutched the stone tightly and remembered what Katla said. "Dark spirit, you do not belong here!" She had seen this work for the exorcist, so it was going to work for her, right? She had to believe.

And then a voice responded. "Alice, whatever is the matter?"

That provided enough of a scare to push through the pressure on her lap and send her practically flying out the door. Katla's magic wasn't effective? And the voice was female, that wasn't what they expected at all. Who was Alice? Was Alice the ghost?

"Calm down, Melanie," Katla tried to comfort as much as she could over the phone call. "I can perform another cleansing of your home. I'll only charge half because the first one didn't take."

"No," protested Mel, "we need a different approach! Asking her to leave didn't work! We need something more dramatic! Can we… can we eliminate her?"

Katla mumbled a bit and replied hesitantly. "The best way to do that is to figure out why she's still here. If you want, I can do some research for you for, say, a hundred a day?"

"I can't live in my house, Katla. She's there! I need an answer faster, or another solution!"

Katla mumbled again. "Okay, okay, let's try talking with her. We'll open a dialogue. I'll bring some more tools over and we'll try a séance."

Dressed in the same over-the-top clothes, Katla walked in the front door again. She gave Mel a slight hug and a kiss on the cheek before pulling more computer equipment from her doctor's bag. This time, in addition to the cameras and the tablet, Katla produced electric candles.

She went immediately to work setting things up in the dining room. Cameras fixed on the table from different angles and the candles were flipped on and placed in a circle around the table's center. In the middle of the circle, Katla placed the stone she had given Mel.

"All right," Katla said with a comforting confidence after flipping off the dining room's light. "We address the spirit of this house. Make yourself known to us."

The candles flicked off and cast the room in darkness. Unfazed, Katla pressed a button on her tablet and turned them back on.

She nodded seriously to Mel. "She's with us. I can feel her presence." Looking to the stone at the table's center, Katla began talking again. "What keeps you in this world, spirit? Who is Alice? Speak to me, I am your voice in the world of the living, let me be your vessel."

A wind blew through the dining room and the heat vanished from the infrared camera feeds. Katla repeated her plea to be the spirit's vessel. The candles went out again. The tablet gave a low battery warning and the screen went black. This left them in total darkness.

Mel heard a frustrated groan from across the table. The voice was Katla's but the faint exotic accent was gone completely from it. "I swore I charged that thing…" There were sounds of fumbling in the darkness and shaking something metal. "Come on, you stupid…"

The candles lit with purple, heatless flames.

Katla screamed so high and so loud that it could've frustrated neighbor's dogs. "W-what the hell?"

"It was too dark," the voice from earlier responded. "Alice could have been hurt."

Katla was frozen utterly motionless, mouth agape and eyes wide with terror.

"Who is Alice?" asked Mel, not seeming to notice Katla's sheer terror. She was finally able to talk to the spirit that had spent weeks now on the edge of making contact.

The purple flames twitched a little. If it was possible to ascribe emotion to them, Mel might've thought they looked confused. "You are, Alice."

Confusion was becoming second nature to Mel, so she gently corrected the spirit instead of being shocked or taken by fear. "My name is Melanie."

The flames dimmed considerably. "I thought you weren't her, but my heart swelled with hopes upon your return here."

"Did Alice hurt you? Is she the one who... who killed you?" Mel wasn't sure she really wanted to know, but she hoped resolving this would help the spirit on her way.

The flames reached near the chandelier at the idea, burning with a momentary fury. "Never!" As the flames settled back to their previous illumination, she continued. "Alice was my life. She was the one who made the birds sing in the morning and the moon shine at night. When I left my body, my greatest crime was leaving my Alice."

This caught Mel off-guard. "Wait... you loved her?"

And then it all clicked. It was the spirit who made her tea. The spirit had tried to welcome Alice back to their home with the message in the mirror. It was a kiss on her neck that made her shiver. It was a head in her lap that paralyzed her.

"You... loved her," Mel repeated, understanding. "And you thought I was her. You weren't trying to hurt me; you were taking care of me."

The flames were barely points of purple light. "You resemble how she did in our youth. And you, too, sought the company of women. You even came to this town, so close to Boston and the seminary. It seemed as though you were looking for me."

"And chasing you off and running from you must've hurt," the guilt overtook Mel. She never once considered that she was missing such a massive piece of the puzzle. "Katla's spells must've offended you, and I'm sorry."

The candle flame looked confused again. "Spells?"

"The banishing and the warding stone," explained Mel.

"It was your desire to be rid of me that hurt, Ali-Melanie. I was not rebuffed by any banishing,"

For the first time since coming face-to-face with a real ghost, Katla sputtered words from her mouth. "No, uh, no refunds."

"But it offends me not that you tried, Melanie," the spirit continued, "because it took great work for me to reach you. You did not know me from Satan himself. Alice, bless her, might have known my touch but you had no reason to. I am ashamed, in truth."

Melanie held her hand out toward the center of the table. "I'm sorry too. Let's meet properly? I'm Melanie Loring, call me Mel."

She felt a slight pressure on the back of her hand, which knowing what she knew now was likely a gentle kiss. "My name is Lydia Ripley."

"Are you going to move on, Lydia?" Mel asked, less eager than she might've been if she hadn't gotten to properly speak to the spirit.

The flames twitched a little and there was a momentary silence. Finally, Lydia answered. "I do not believe I can."

"Are you afraid? Of judgment?" Katla was finally able to speak.

"No," responded the spirit. "I am afraid of not being here should Alice return." The tongues of the flames all pointed at Katla intensely. "Are you afraid of judgment, my medium?"

"So that's the story," explained Mel to the small camera on her laptop. "It turns out Lydia needs a lot of energy to do things in our world, so I keep a travel charger plugged in for her when she needs it. We're actually friends now, strange as it seems. We're learning. Her about everything she's missed while haunting this old house and me about what kind of person she was, and who Alice was."

"Why are we doing this?" Lydia's voice whispered. Mel wasn't sure if the microphone would pick it up or not, but she hoped it would.

Mel looked to where she heard the voice coming from. "So if you ever find her, you won't forget this part of the story. And so if someone else is afraid of you, they can know you. People only fear what they don't know, right?"

"That medium may beg to differ," the voice had a note of caution.

Mel nodded, "And odds are whoever watches this will just call me crazy, I know." She couldn't help but smile, though. "I like my kind of crazy, Lydia."

And her kind of crazy liked her too.

About the Author

Katelyn Cameron is a writer from Kalamazoo, Michigan. She's written a few short stories focused heavily on women-loving-women in science fiction and fantasy spaces. She also shepherds a community of roleplayers in online games, presents panels about women-loving-women-centric stories at pop culture conventions, and loves cosplay. She's been published in Queeromance Ink's flash fiction collections and A Heart Well Traveled by Sapphire Books.

The Other War

By Monica Schultz

Florence Taylor is on the run. Abandoning her life in Australia, she volunteers as a nurse in the Western Front of World War One.
Georgie Taylor is searching for his older sister. She's all he has left, but following her into the war could be too risky.
As the war closes in around them and spies lurk in the shadows, it's only a matter of time before their family secret is revealed to the human world.

I wake with a gasp, my hands flying to my chest, my heart thundering. Visions of the Human Protection Society, the organization that controls the last mythical population on earth, slowly fade. They sneak through the stacks of supply crates, their long, white lab coats hiding weapons ineffective against humans. I squeeze my eyes shut, gulp down the bile rising in my throat, and take a deep breath. I'm safe.

As my heart slows, I peer through the gap in the back canopy. Desolate land, pocked by shell fire and burnt to a crisp, rushes past our truck. *Thud.* I slam against the metal frame of the truck. Groaning, I rub my shoulder before pounding a fist against the headboard.

"Hey, watch it, mate!" I yell at Jones.

No response, but I'm not surprised. The engines in these army trucks are deafening, it's a wonder Jones can even hear his radio. Besides, it wasn't his idea that got me into this mess. It took hours of begging and false promises for Jones to even consider letting me catch a ride with him this morning. Now I'm miles away, slipping just out of reach before the Society's scattered spies can find me.

I exhale, tension rushing from my body like the air leaving a balloon. Wriggling my back against a crate, I make myself more comfortable on the vibrating floor of the truck. Lines of sweat trickle down my spine, gluing my stiff nurse's uniform to my skin. Summer in Europe is nothing compared to the hair-frizzing humidity of Australia, but the inside of this truck has become a furnace. The air that slithers through the canvas roof does nothing to cool the rapidly heating metal tray.

Despite the stench of petrol filling my nose, my stomach growls. I lay a hand against my growing middle, gently stroking it. There must be something to eat in all these crates. Too unsteady to get to my feet, I crawl from crate to crate, squinting at the labels. *Vêtements, médicament, boeuf traité*. If only I had bothered to learn some French before enlisting. Following my nose, I claw my way into the *boeuf traité* crate and dig out a cool, square tin. Cracking it open, I grimace. Bullied beef. I pinch my nose and tip my head back, swallowing the entire contents in three quick chews. Rations with their salty preservatives can never compare to pack meals back home; the perfect fresh cuts of meat and steaming plates full of vegetables. Yet, they are enough to fuel a human soldier.

Distracted by my hunger, I don't realize the truck has stopped until Jones pulls aside the canvas flap, and I am bathed in sunlight.

"What is *this*, Private?" a stick-thin woman demands, shaking her finger at me.

I quickly tuck the tin into my pocket and wipe the sweat from my brow. The beef crate lies on its side, its contents spilling across the back of the truck. I gulp. This is not the first impression I was hoping for.

"You brought me a stowaway!" She yells, her brow wrinkling into a stern valley. Greying curls slip from beneath her nurse's cap, lining her oddly familiar face.

"Sister Kent, I assure you Miss Taylor is here on official business," Jones says, his shoulders stiff, hands clenched by his sides. My tongue sticks to the roof of my mouth, glued there as my brain empties of thought. I wait for Jones to say more, leaning towards him. The Private clears his throat and tilts his head ever so slightly towards Sister Kent.

Oh.

I jump to my feet, dusting off the crumbs of my meal. Reaching into my bulging pocket, I bypass the incriminating tin and withdraw my crumpled orders from Doctor Wright.

"Forgive me, Sister. My name is… um, it is Mary Taylor." I lie, momentarily forgetting what name I had used at my last hospital. "Doctor Wright gave me leave just yesterday to join the nurses at your Casualty Clearing Station, but… well, I always believe it is best to be early, so I came on the first supply truck."

The hastily smoothed orders tremble as I hold them aloft. I force myself to smile, silently begging the heavens for her to accept my lame excuse.

Sister Kent's beady eyes narrow.

"A stowaway who cannot remember her own name," she huffs. "Very well, I know what to do with you. Carry on, Private."

Sister Kent straightens, snatching the orders from my hand and heading off down the dusty track towards the tents.

With a shaky smile to Jones, I jump off the truck and scramble to catch up with Sister Kent's quick march. As we pass between simple canvas tents, I struggle to ignore my aching legs, the muscles stretching out after the long drive. Grateful to be moving, I swallow mouthfuls of fresh air only to gag on new foul odors. Even outside, the station reeks of blood and decay, worse than any emergency hospital I've worked in.

"Glad you're here?" Sister Kent says with a smirk as I cough. "You young ones always beg to be closer to our boys, then faint the moment you get 'ere."

Sister Kent halts before the largest of the tents and I crash into her back. I stumble backward, apologizing profusely.

"Listen 'ere now. Every bedpan in this tent better be spotless by noon, or you can forget about your midday meal with the mess you made of my rations."

My stomach rumbles, "But-"

"No buts," Sister Kent scolds, flicking back the tent flap with a bony hand. "Now get on with it."

I bite my tongue, my eyes flickering heavenwards. The sun is already inching towards its peak.

I bow my head, resigned, "Yes, Sister Kent."

****

Rancid air, thick with the musk of sweat, clouds the tent. The floor is naked dirt, stamped smooth by hundreds of soldiers in their march across the Western Front. The tent flap closes with a swish, sealing me in.

I head straight for the first occupied bed, reaching for his bedpan silently, my stomach swirling with nausea. His tired eyes stare silently at a distant point above him, straining to stay open despite the monotony of the tent. I glance over my shoulder, checking for signs of the white nurses' uniform. We're alone.

Pushing back my fear of punishment, I draw the solider out of his daze.

"Hello there," I whisper, my voice soft and coaxing, "My name's Mary, what's yours?"

The soldier stares at me in a daze, shaking his head softly in disbelief.

"Winston," the soldier croaks, his throat dry from disuse.

I offer Winston water from my flask, watching him drink as I collect his bedpan. Once Winston quenches his thirst, I ask after his injuries, checking if there is anything more I can do for him. For Winston, and many others, my friendly face is enough to ease his pain. I continue working in this way for several beds, slowing my cleaning to stir laughter in the wounded. The effect is immediate; chatter filling the previously silent tent. Their pale skin now shines with color and forgetting their pain for a moment. I grin. Our men need comfort more than a sterile toilet.

The next bedframe over rattles as a soldier stirs in his sleep. He screams, and I freeze in my tracks, watching as he bats at invisible enemies. The sound cuts through the room, stirring distant memories as it rings in my ears. *Georgie?*

My throat constricting, I rush to him.

"Georgie!" I cry, hiccupping as tears spring to my eyes, "Oh, Georgie, you're okay."

My hands reach out for him, stroking the mess of his once soft auburn locks.

Georgie's startling sapphire eyes fly open. A sprinkling of freckles dusts his long, crooked nose, broken thrice from wrestling with our cousins. Looking at my kid brother is like staring into a mirror. I cup his cheek, feeling the scratch of scattered stubble.

"Flossy," Georgie smiles revealing his sharp canines and dimpled cheeks. "My beard's finally coming in," he laughs softly, the sound quickly developing into a deep, rattling cough.

I prop Georgie up on his pillows, holding his shoulders as he struggles to breathe. A tear slips down my cheek as he gulps down the flask of water I pass him.

"Oh heavens, Georgie, what have you done to yourself?"

My hand trembles as it hovers over his mummified feet.

"It's nothing Flossy," Georgie winces as he pulls himself further upright, "Just a touch of trench foot."

"Nothing! George William Taylor, you shouldn't even be here." Glancing over my shoulder, I dare to raise my voice above a whisper, "How could they let you fight? You don't look a day over sixteen!"

"Says you! I wouldn't have enlisted if you didn't run off first! What were you thinking? Risking everything to chase after some scrawny human who couldn't even beat you in a thumb wrestle. Let alone protect your hide like a true mate," Georgie snaps, poking me where he knows it hurts.

I growl in return, my arm hairs bristling. My ears prick as wounded soldiers whisper to each other, craning their necks. The pack gives me enough grief over Arthur as it is, and they don't even know half as much as Georgie. I lean over him, struggling to lower my voice.

"You know nothing," I spit, my gums aching as my teeth lengthen, "I had to go. It was the only way to stay safe from the Society."

Georgie's chest heaves as he pants in his bed, fists clenched by his sides. "I'm not some kid anymore!"

"Georgie!" I snap, my eyes nervously skittering across the room, "Keep your voice down."

"You can't lie to me and pretend the Society hasn't forbidden mythical involvement in the war effort. You were safe in Australia! Here you're just a sitting duck," Georgie rages, ignoring me.

My eyes burn as my vision dims to grey. Cursing, I squeeze my eyes shut and swallow my pride. No, not here. Not now. My eyes open, catching the bewitched stares of dozens of soldiers. Georgie gasps, realizing what I have moments before him.

In control of myself once more, I press my hand against Georgie's burning forehead, heedless of our audience.

"Shh, Georgie, it's okay," I soothe, even as panic fills my chest. Georgie's eyes rove beneath his lids, his body twitching.

"Come now, you've made it this far. Think of what Uncle Pat taught us. You're stronger than the full moon. Your will is fiercer than the wildest emotion."

Slowly, Georgie stills, sweat streaming down his temples. I dab the sweat with the edge of my sleeve, murmuring nonsense until his breathing deepens.

"They haven't found you then?" Georgie asks, his voice strained.

I shake my head fiercely. "They won't, I promise."

Georgie lies back against his pillows, "I reckon they don't have as many spies as people say. Nobody said a thing during my first full moon."

I sigh, my shoulders sagging with fatigue. If only I could believe him. Yet twice now I have fled, the threat of discovery hard on my heels.

"Maybe…" I murmur, squeezing Georgie's hand in mine as his eyes slowly sink shut. Resisting transformation takes a severe toll, especially for someone so young.

"Miss Taylor!" I jump in my skin, turning to face Sister Kent. She storms towards us, a filthy bedpan in hand, "One task, Miss Taylor, and I come back to find you canoodling with our patients!"

I hold my ground, my head held high, "I'm doing my job. You've severely neglected these men. A little smile and some kindness can change a person's life."

Sister Kent shakes her head, her mouth opening, ready to reprimand me, then her eyes land on Georgie who startles awake once more. A slow, cruel smile spreads across her face as her eyes flicker from Georgie to me. With one swift motion, she clutches Georgie's chin between her bony fingers as she tilts his head from side to side. Shivers race down my spine as I struggle to hold myself still.

"I see what this is about. A family reunion," Sister Kent drops Georgie's chin, her fingers leaving red marks on his face. "Miss Taylor, you should know it won't be long before we ship these men off to a hospital further west. In such a place as this, we cannot afford to waste time on those who are no longer on the brink of death; even if a nurse wishes to stay close to her brother."

I glare at Sister Kent, perfectly understanding her meaning. With one last tight squeeze of Georgie's hand, I let him go. I can only pray Sister Kent is stupid enough to believe I'm incapable of securing transfers to Georgie's new hospital. Eager for Sister Kent to leave, I attempt to snatch the blasted bedpan away, only for her to hold it out of reach.

"Not so fast, Miss Taylor. I won't have you wasting my time any longer. You will take the fouled bed linen and wash them out back." Sister Kent kicks the bedpan under Georgie's bed, the slosh of its contents the only sound in the room. While her back is turned, I mouth sorry to the remaining patients, abandoned once again, and plant a kiss on Georgie's cheek. I promise myself, this won't be the last time I see him.

****

My stomach aches as I tip another bucket of murky water onto the trampled grass, transforming the hard earth to mud. True to her word, Sister Kent ensures I receive no mid-day rations to fuel my growing body.

At first, stubbornness provides me the strength to beat the stains out of the bedsheets, but as the sun sinks lower in the sky, my arms grow weary and my hands smart from bleach. I stretch, rubbing the ache in the small of my back as I listen to the wind. A cool breeze sweeps through the station, carrying with it the echoing booms of the front line. It flutters through the fresh white linen, hanging from a rope strung between two tents.

I hear the whistle of a shell speeding past the tents, moments before it lands with an explosive crash that sends me sprawling in the dirt. Shielding my face, I crawl towards the nearest tent and out of the open. My heart hammers in my chest as a siren blares to life, its shrieking call ringing in my ears. I whimper, clamping my hands over my ears to drown out the immobilizing sound. It isn't enough. I groan, curling into a ball as the siren splits my head in two. The wolf in me begs for release, to protect my sensitive human ears with thick fur. I squeeze my eyes shut, blocking out the rush of people scrambling for cover.

"Nurse Taylor?" A hoarse voice calls over the thunderous crash of shells.

I blink through the pain, forcing my eyes to focus on the man that crouches before me. He crosses himself, gazing heavenward as he says a quick prayer. A padre. Reassured by his weapon-less belt, I let his hands gently circle my shoulders, lifting my quivering body off the ground.

"Lord bless you; you must be our new nurse." I watch the padre's mustache twitch above his lips as he speaks, my ringing ears struggling to catch his words. I shake my head violently until the only sound that remains is a dull buzz.

"Can you hear me, Nurse Taylor?" Although he holds me upright, the padre's voice is distant. Concern lines his face, forming tight wrinkles behind his spectacles. "All medical staff are to retreat to the dugouts."

I pull free of his grip, stumbling wildly. *Focus*, I scold myself. With a wince, I prod my ear gently. Thick, dark blood coats my fingertips. If only I could change, my body would repair itself in an instant. Shaking off my bleak thoughts, I scent the air, lifting my nose to the wind. The station reeks of terror, wafting from the tents in pungent clouds. My eyes grow wide as realization hits me. Georgie needs me.

The padre's face is grim as he watches me. His eyes speak of countless men and women who have succumbed to shell shock, believing I'm one of them.

"Nurse Taylor, we must leave. It's not safe."

I shake my head once more. *What is unsafe for us is lethal for the crippled soldiers bound to their beds.* My mind made up, I rip his spectacles off his head and snap the thin frames between my growing claws. The padre shouts, dropping to the ground to pick up the shattered pieces.

"Forgive me, Padre," I call over my shoulder as I sprint away. I dart between tents, leaving a winding trail back to Georgie no blind man could follow. Hot on Georgie's scent, my nose and jaw lengthen into a grotesque snout, distorting my human face. My ears twitch as they grow to sharp points and fill with the overwhelming cacophony of war. Adrenaline courses through my veins, allowing me to run harder and faster than before. I hurdle over tent ropes, my teeth clenched to still the howl that begs for release. Skidding to a halt, I pant before Georgie's tent. I gulp down deep breaths of air, pressing on my nose until I am sure I won't petrify the humans with my monstrous appearance.

"Flossy!" Georgie's scream shatters through my deaf ears and jolts me to action. Throwing caution to the wind, I burst through the tent flaps, Georgie's name on my lips. The tent is in chaos. Soldiers cower on the floor beneath the thin metal frames of their beds. Trays of cleaning and medical supplies lie strewn across the ground, scattered as the wounded struggled to protect themselves. My scalp prickles as I meet the eyes of patients I tended to earlier this morning. They tremble at the sight of me, unable to meet my fierce gaze. Their heads turn away, all looking towards the bed frame on its side.

"Georgie?" I whisper hesitantly, as I creep around the side of the bed. A low whimper replies. Georgie withers on the floor, mid-transformation, his body contorting as it resists his base instincts. His back arches, auburn fur exploding through his thin patient's gown. Tears pool in the black markings that edge Georgie's eyes and spill across his muzzle as he releases a pitiful, hollow whine.

His body shaking, Georgie limps to his feet. Bandages pool around his back legs, revealing raw and blistered paws. Despite the stench of fear growing to a suffocating miasma as the wounded watch Georgie in horror, I smile. Hair rapidly regrows over his paws, mending in seconds the wounds which immobilized his human form.

Transfixed by Georgie, I don't see the knife until it's too late. A flash of silver flickers through the air and lodges itself into Georgie's flank. We turn as one, facing the threat. Sister Kent crouches behind a bedframe, a knife glinting in her clenched fist. I growl in warning; the sound rumbling through my body as Sister Kent raises the knife above her head. Sister Kent freezes, her eyes flickering from me to Georgie.

"You don't want to do that," I say as calmly as I can, raising my open hands, "I promise he won't hurt you, so long as you drop the knife."

"Won't hurt me!" Sister Kent laughs, but the sound is thin and humorless. "The pup couldn't hurt me if he tried. I know how you *beasts* react to silver."

My mouth drops in horror. I peek at Georgie from the corner of my eye, not daring to turn from Sister Kent. Blood flows from Georgie's flank, matting his fur and turning the earth beneath his paws to mud. Georgie trembles, breaking eye contact with Sister Kent to lick his wound. At the sight of Georgie's submission, my rage burns to life. I inch forwards, keeping Georgie behind me.

"Not another step!" Sister Kent yells, holding the knife aloft. She presses her lips together, her eyes filled with absolute disgust. I pause. I've seen that exact look before. Dread's fingers wrap around my heart, squeezing until the life drains from my face.

"You're with the Society," I whisper, as her face clicks into place in my memories. A stern glance from a nurse who I dismissed as just another human now shines brightly as a warning sign for the hospitals I would flee from.

Sister Kent grins, straightening with pride. "I should have known you were a mythical the moment you arrived, Mary Taylor – if that is even your name. I must admit you're cleverer than others to avoid revealing yourself for so long. Yet the Society always prevails. You *will* die here for your disobedience."

My mind races. The Society is explicit in their ban of mythical enlistments in the Great War. Sister Kent's eyes gleam as she hurls the second knife. It slices through the air, hilt over tip, as if moving through honey. I dive to cover Georgie, adrenaline masking my pain as my bones splinter and hastily reshape. My uniform drops from my body in ribbons as I catch the knife between my canines. I spit the blade out, bile burning my throat as my tongue blisters.

With a low growl, I turn to Sister Kent, whose mouth hangs open as she stumbles backward. I leap, my fur rippling as my muscles tense.

We crash into the tent, tearing a gaping hole in the wall. Sister Kent gasps, the air knocked out of her lungs as she rolls out from under me. I snap my jaws, lunging for her, but she's slippery, crawling out of reach at the last moment. Silver glints as Sister Kent reaches for another knife, hidden under her white dress. My eyes lock onto the knife as fear and adrenaline charge through my veins. Yet even with the haze of my emotions, a quiet voice speaks. I mustn't hurt her.

The Society will not twist me into the monster they think I am.

My ears press flat against my skull as my mind races. I dart forwards, baring teeth. I nip arms, legs, anything to distract and confuse Sister Kent. Too close. My shoulder burns as the blade hacks off a chunk of fur that I cannot heal. A snarl rips through my body. She flinches, and I press my advantage.

Quick on my feet, I rush her from behind. My teeth hook into the grey curls at the nape of her neck. She screams and bats at my head wildly, but I hold steady. With a sharp jerk, I yank her off her feet and fling her to the ground. She lands with a thump, her limbs falling limp. I pant, watching anxiously to see if she will rise.

Nothing. I whine, creeping forward. Sister Kent's chest swells with air. I breathe a sigh of relief. Crouched, I slink over to her and sniff. Fear no longer clouds her scent. My tail untucks. Humans are terrible at concealing their base emotions.

I cock my head, my ears twisting to catch the howl of a shell as it hurtles overhead and crashes in the distance. Yet the tent is silent. Wind whistles through the hole as I clamber inside. Georgie lies on his side, panting heavily. He licks my chin as I stand over him and survey the room. Soldiers watch us with wide eyes from the corners of the tent and the underside of beds. They quake, their hands over their heads, unsure which poses the greater threat; a wounded wolf or the distant shells.

Turning my back to them, I lie beside Georgie, pressing my head against his to share my warmth. His eyes speak volumes. The Georgie I know is nowhere in sight; the wolf is in control. I hum softly, licking Georgie's face all over to mask my true fear. But it's no use. I don't even have the courage to face his wound yet. Especially not as a wolf, with my every thought laid out for Georgie to see.

Squeezing my eyes shut, I focus my strength on my human soul within. I continue to hum as my fur retracts, disappearing beneath my soft skin. My fingers curl as my knuckles crunch. Claws shrink to nails. I shiver, curling into a tight ball as my muscles tremble with fatigue. The cold air stings my shoulder as blood trickles down my pale freckled arm and drips to the floor. I moan, but crawl through the pain, scooting until I am facing Georgie's flank. Pressing my hands against his soaked fur, I stem the flow of blood. My eyes search the floor, scanning for a cloth to act as a compress.

"Here, Miss," a soldier stands over us, his eyes averted as he holds out a bundle of bandages with one hand, the other tied up in a sling. He's short and hunches at the waist, shifting from foot to foot as he stares at everything but me. My cheeks burn as I realize my current state. Nudity is common among the pack, but Uncle always joked about the prudish nature of human society.

"Thank you," I murmur, accepting the bandages. I hunch my shoulders in a weak attempt to conceal my breasts, but it is no use. With a deep breath, I clutch the hilt of the knife and slide it out, covering the gash with the bandages. Blood blooms across the white fabric, drenching it in seconds. My stomach rolls. I glance back up at the soldier who watches with his lips pressed together.

"I need a needle and thread," I whisper around the lump in my throat. He nods and disappears from my side. I comb my free hand through Georgie's fur, murmuring sweet nonsense. He closes his eyes, breathing steadily through his nose.

"Please, Georgie," I plead, my voice cracking as I struggle to speak. Tears cloud my eyes as I gulp. Werewolves cannot heal wounds delivered by silver. Georgie's only chance is to return to human form, but, consumed by pain, the wolf runs wild in his heart.

"Is there anything else?" the soldier asks, concern lacing his voice. The needle and thread dangle from his hand as he holds it just out of my reach.

I shake my head, not trusting myself to speak. Swallowing my nerves, I pull aside the bandages, my hands shaking.

"I can help if he'll let me," he says, nodding towards Georgie as he crouches by my side.

My mouth drops open, a protest about his age coming to my lips, but he is surely no younger than I am. I bite my lip, my eyes trained on Georgie.

"Please Miss, they had me working as a medic in the field. I don't need my other hand to stitch."

I squeeze my eyes shut until the tears drip down my cheeks. With a resigned sigh, I shuffle out of the way, letting him take my place. I crawl to Georgie's head, pressing a kiss against his thick fur as I take his head in my hands. The soldier watches us intently, inching closer to Georgie's flank. Georgie's lip curls back, revealing deadly canines as he growls.

"Hush, Georgie, let…"

"Ernest," the soldier says, filling my silence.

"… Ernest help you. I can't do it alone this time."

Georgie drops his head onto my lap, the fight fading from his eyes. His wet nose presses against my swollen stomach, his hot breath warming my skin. Georgie tenses and I know the needle has pricked his skin.

"Done," Ernest says, and I release a breath I didn't know I was holding.

Georgie shivers, his eyes rolling back in their sockets as his body finally relaxes. Beneath my fingers, Georgie's skull softens and reshapes. Thick fur curls to a head-full of auburn ringlets. Georgie's eyes shine as he lifts his face from my bare legs. But then he looks at me, really looks, and his jaw drops.

"You're pregnant." Georgie rests a hand against my stomach, feeling the curve of the child growing within. I hold his hand there, terrified of letting go.

"You see now why I had to go?" My eyes search his, tears brimming until I can no longer see.

"Flossy," Georgie starts, grimacing as he pulls himself upright, "You will be a wonderful Mother." He holds my face in both his hands, a grin replacing the pain in his eyes. "You practically raised me and look at us now."

I choke out a laugh, covering my mouth with my hand.

Ernest clears his throat and we turn in unison. He stares at his bare feet, his cheeks bright red.

"Miss..." Ernest says, holding out a used sheet torn from a bed. I smile, wiping the tears from my eyes as Georgie drapes the sheet protectively around us. Georgie shuffles closer, wrapping me in his arms as if I'm the one with a jagged gash down my side, not a child growing in my stomach. Closing my eyes, I rest my head against his warm chest and sigh. My shoulders drop, finally releasing the burden that I have been carrying alone for far too long.

Taking in my surroundings, I look out at the tent from Georgie's embrace like a child peeking between the gaps between their parent's fingers. Slowly, soldiers rise to their feet and whisper to those bed-bound. One by one those who can creep closer, remaining far from Georgie's reach. They speak to Ernest in hushed tones, gesturing wildly to the tent roof, which has miraculously withstood the shelling. I squeeze Georgie's hand and he nods. *Escape.* The word lingers on both our minds, our wolf's senses reminding us that there is no safety among humans.

Yet the thought comes too late. Sister Kent stumbles through the gap in the tent, a filthy, dirt-smeared knife gripped in her fist.

"Stupid, useless girl," she mutters, swaying on her feet, her eyes glassy, "You couldn't even snap my neck!"

I climb to my feet, facing her with a glare.

"I didn't try."

Georgie hurries to follow me, blood snaking its way down his leg as he twists. He stands between us, lifting the sheet I had let fall, hiding my stomach from Sister Kent's keen eyes.

"Honour," Georgie booms, his voice filling the room, "Werewolves are mythicals of honor. We do not fight to kill the weak and vulnerable." I look up at my little brother in wonder, my heart swelling with pride.

"Weak? Vulnerable?" Sister Kent sputters, fury masking her better judgment, "Boy do you know who I am? The Human Protection Society controls you."

Georgie holds up a hand, his gaze level and steady as he stares at Sister Kent.

"The Society is nothing," he says in a voice I never knew he had. "We have bested you. Now stand aside and let us be."

"Never," Sister Kent spits, even as she leans against a nearby bedframe. Voices fill the room as the soldiers share their confusion, their eyes glued to us.

"Enough," Ernest steps between Georgie and Sister Kent, glancing towards me as if for permission.

After a moment's hesitation, I nod.

"Whoever you say you are, these two have done you no wrong. Werewolves..." Ernest starts then stops himself, shaking his head. "Who would have thought a nurse throwing knives at a boy is more disgusting than a having a hundred-pound wolf in my tent?"

"This doesn't concern you," Sister Kent slurs, stumbling forwards. As one, the soldiers mimic her movement, tightening into a circle around Georgie and me.

Ernest glances from his mates to Sister Kent, a confident smile coming to his lips. With practiced ease, he rests a hand on Georgie's shoulder, though I can smell him sweating anxiously. "Black or white, werewolf or not, a fella who fights to protect our land from those stinkin' Germans *is* my concern."

My heart soars as soldiers cheer, clapping Ernest on. I grin, delighting as Sister Kent's mouth opens and shuts like a fish out of water, as she struggles to find her words.

"Nurse Taylor! Sister Kent!" the padre shouts, his voice still distant in the now quiet station.

"We can make you a hero," I whisper, my mind working quickly to gather the scraps of an escape plan. "The Society needn't know you found us, or what truly happened today."

Sister Kent frowns, resting her heavy head in her hands, "But there are too many witnesses. They can't know the truth… that people like you exist."

"Who will believe a handful of shell-shocked, trench survivors?" Ernest suggests, and I nod along with the others.

"Listen, your name could go down in history as the woman who sacrificed her own safety to provide courage to our men during bombardment…" I let my words dangle in the air, pausing even as I hear the padre drawing closer. "Or you can remain forever another faceless spy for the Society. Your choice."

Sister Kent trembles, then collapses to her knees, bowing her blood-stained head in defeat. Georgie and I share a quick glance, our sapphire eyes mirroring each other's thoughts. Now's our chance. Dropping the sheet, I plant a kiss on Ernest's cheek, my body shimmering before his eyes. I fall to all fours, my ears twitching as they listen for the padre. Trusting the soldiers to remain as loyal as the wolf, we turn our backs and disappear with the wind through the hole in the tent.

About the Author

Monica Schultz is a High School Mathematics teacher from Ipswich, Australia, with a passion for writing urban and historical fantasy. Her short fiction is published in various Australian and international anthologies. When she isn't writing or teaching, Monica enjoys curling up with her cat and a good book. She dreams of one day publishing her young adult novel so she can share it with her students.

Visit her website below for upcoming works or follow her on Instagram @monicaschultzauthor for updates on life's madness.

https://monicaschultzauthor.weebly.com/

And the Windows Shook

By C. Marry Hultman

As the world crashes around them, Sanna and Emma are trapped inside their school while otherworldly ghouls wait to kill them.

There was a loud sound. It seemed to reverberate through the floor and climbed, like ripples on water, up the walls and then across the ceiling, causing the lamps to swing. Sanna looked up from her microscope, greeted by flickering lights. She rubbed her eyes, waiting for the aftershock, tilting her head to the side like a dog waiting for the next command from its master, but there was only the quiet hum of the laboratory fan. The background noise she had grown accustomed to in room 221. Either it had gotten darker outside already and more time had passed than she thought or incessantly staring at bacteria in a petri dish had messed her up.

She blinked to adjust herself to the surroundings but to no avail. She scooted across the chairs, neatly standing in a row, the way she liked it, until her body was next to the window. It was dusky outside. Big purple clouds billowing like smoke from a bonfire moved erratically across the dark sky. It looked more like October than May.

"Did you feel that?" she asked the figure quietly reading poetry at the other end of the room. There was no reply. "Emma!" Sanna called and managed to get the attention of her friend.

"What?" Emma looked up. "What are you on about?"

"Didn't you feel that?"

"Feel what?" Emma used her voice to show her disinterest in Sanna's concerns. This happened quite a bit since Sanna often had concerns, but Emma had learned to feign interest, to avoid conflicts. In return, Sanna had learned not to take the mock interest as an insult. It was why their friendship worked.

"There was some kind of crash" Sanna replied. "Maybe an earthquake. Whatever it was, it was quite violent."

"Well, I didn't feel anything" Emma put down the book and swung her legs from the desk with a pained expression. "My legs are asleep so I doubt I can sense anything at all from the waist down."

Sanna smirked and jumped down from her chair. Her legs were also stiff from sitting in front of the microscope for several hours. Ever since school had let out around four.

"You done for today?" Emma asked as they converged at the head of the classroom.

"I believe I have gotten as much as humanly possible out of staring at growths today" Sanna started unbuttoning the lab coat and smoothed out her plaid skirt underneath.

"Don't you feel that it's unfair that you are sitting here, burning the candle at both ends while the others are sitting at home?" Emma put away the microscope and tossed the petri dish to her friend.

"I don't mind" Sanna awkwardly caught the dish by smashing it against her body. "The other two are supposed to do the research part and I really don't feel like having my nose buried in dull books."

To her, it was a great compromise. She had neither patience nor the focus to sift through pages of other people's production. She was well aware of her own limitations. How her brain would sometimes feel as if it was on fire and whenever that happened she was incapable of getting anything done. *Her mind was a labyrinth and while the parts of her brain were clearly comprehensible, its ways deceptively apparent, its destinations were unknown, its secrets still secrets.*

The small indicator on her phone was blinking maniacally in the dark, sitting atop the round table outside the lab. She assumed it was Mother desperately trying to contact her. It must be later than she thought for her mother to call.

"What time is it, Emma?" she asked before lifting the device from the table.

"My phone is dead, but the clock on the wall says it's eight. Why?"

"I think my mom's been calling."

"Well, she might have tried to call me instead then." The two of them always stuck together, and if you were looking for one, you might as well call the other.

Sanna woke the phone. There were five missed calls, all from the same person – not her mother, though. "Maja's called," she said and raised an eyebrow. "She's called me five times the past half hour."

"That's odd," Emma replied, this time with interest. "I wonder what could be that important."

Sanna hit the call button and put the phone to her ear. The signal stuttered a bit as it rang and after a short while, there was an answer.

"Hello," Sanna began. "Maja?" There was static and crackling. Maja's voice came in and out, only allowing single syllables to break through, and then the line went dead.

"What did she want?" Emma asked, readying herself to leave.

"I don't know" Sanna slowly lowered the phone. "The reception was terrible. Odd if she's in town. My bars are full."

"If it's important she'll call back. Let's head home."

Sanna nodded, but there was something not quite right. There was an uneasy feeling deep in her stomach. It was difficult to say what it was doing there, or what it was telling her, but it was there.

Walking through the silent corridors of Slinger High School was always eerie. Sanna failed to put her finger on why. It could be she had always thought to herself, that it went against the natural order of things. High school hallways were supposed to be bustling with life. Young adults heading to various classes, discussing school dances, Netflix shows, or prospective partners. All the while carrying their books close to their chests and backpacks slung over one shoulder. She would be the first to admit her ideal world was more like a high school movie, but in truth Slinger High School rather was and it made her reality work. Dark corridors where only the footsteps of two teenagers echoing were audible did the opposite in her mind.

"I guess there are others who are up late," Emma remarked as they passed the school library. Through the large windows, they could clearly see the glow from a light somewhere in the recesses of the shelves.

"Probably Nick" Sanna said and snickered. Nick was a former student who had previously held the position of student body president before her. He had so loved school and the status it brought, that the teachers had joked that he would never leave. He had shown them all by getting a job as the school librarian and thus proved them all correct. Who had won out of that exchange was of constant debate among the students.

"That, or Maja" Emma suggested. "She's been spending quite a bit of time in there lately."

As if on cue, Sanna's phone rang and Maja's name appeared on the screen. They both smiled at the coincidence. When Sanna answered, static crackled in her ear while she strained to understand her friend.

Emma tried to follow the conversation as Sanna walked back and forth with a finger in one ear and the phone in the other. It was apparent that she was struggling to understand, while also trying to speak.

"What's going on?" Emma asked as her friend suddenly put down her phone.

"I'm not quite sure" Sanna tried to dial Maja's number again, but nothing happened. "She wanted to know where we were, and when I told her, she urged me to stay indoors. To stay here until the sun comes up. She kept yelling stay inside."

"Why?"

"Who knows, but whatever it is, she felt it was important. Then she said to get up on the roof. We'd understand once we were on the roof."

"The roof?"

Emma knew exactly how to get to the roof. She took photos for The Night Crier, the school paper, and her editor was adamant she get a cool picture of the Slinger skyline. They circled a corner of lockers to head up the stairs when they heard the unmistakable screeching of tires, followed by virulent banging on glass.

They quickly moved in the opposite direction, eyeing each other with concern. As they came closer to the main entrance, the desperate banging on the glass intensified, and a tall, silhouetted figure was visible against the glass.

"You go on, I'll hang back here" Emma halted and leaned on the lockers.

Sanna glanced at her, never ceasing her movement. Her heart threatened to beat right out of her chest and her knitted sweater was drenched with perspiration. She could not quite grip the situation. It was going against the very fabric of her being. Something was drawing her to open up the door for a complete stranger. What did the fact that they were safe inside mean? Was everyone else not? Her mother, brother, friends. Were they safe inside? She reached the doors, fumbled with the keys. She refused to look at was going on outside, it would only paralyze her. She found the right set of keys shoved it into the lock and turned. The door flew open and pushed her back into Emma standing behind her. The figure slammed the doors shut and turned the key still in place before collapsing against it.

Emma held Sanna in her arms, holding her steady as they watched the young man. His ragged breath breaking the silence. On the other side of the glass doors, several other shapes appeared. They stepped up in a row with their faces only inches from the doors so that the light from overhead illuminated them. It gave their eyes a hollow and sickly visage. In the dark recesses of their sockets, pinpoints of greenish light glowed like cats' eyes reflecting the headlights of a car on a dark autumn night. Their faces bore wide grins, revealing too many rows of teeth. Their skin was melting off their bodies. Blistering and oozing as if it was boiling underneath and they were all covered in a green sheen. Some wore T-Shirts or tank tops and the exposed skin looked diseased and sallow. In their hands, they carried what looked like large porcupine quills. They began tapping them against the glass.

Tap-Tap-tap

In unison

Tap-tap-tap

As one

Tap-tap-tap

Their eyes fixated on them

Tap-tap-tap

Wide grins getting wider

The young man backed away from the door, shaking with fear.

"Get the fuck away from me, you freaks!" He cried at the group.

Tap-tap-tap

He turned to Emma and Sanna, and they recognized him as Adam. In Sanna's need to categorize people and things into her high school movie world, he was one of the popular kids. Handsome, wealthy, and athletic. She had classes with him and she reckoned he was smart as well, but way too lazy to care. What perturbed her was that he did not engage in any school sports. A young man of his build; lean and muscular, and stellar good looks would have been perfect as the quarterback of the school football team (*Go Owls!*), but he was not. It was disrupting her circles.

"Who is that?" He shone the torch from his cell phone at them. Once he recognized their squinting faces, he lowered the light. "Are you guys all good?"

"What do you mean?" Emma asked and looked down on herself to see if he had spotted something on her.

"Your skin's not melting or oozing?" Adam raised an eyebrow and cautiously moved closer to them.

"Not that we've noticed," Sanna said in an offended tone, still distracted by the tapping on the glass behind him.

"Good, good" Adam continued. "Then you seem legit. We need to turn on the lights in the building."

"Why?" Emma began when the tapping suddenly stopped. Adam turned to the entrance.

One of the men had stepped out of the lineup and had sidled up to the glass doors. The beady pinpoints of his eyes were fixated on a point behind them as if he was looking through them rather than at them. With a soft squelch, he placed his forehead on the glass, greenish beads of sweat rolling down the surface bathed in the yellow glow from the overhead lights. He placed a twisted hand on the glass, palm as damp as the rest of him.

"You can hide in there as much as you like" the voice coming from the man was low and gravely. "We are surrounding the building and we will find a way inside, and when we do you and your little friends will meet the sharp end like those other ones."

****

Adam took a few steps closer, moving slowly. Sanna tried to follow, but Emma placed a hand on her shoulder.

"Or you could let us in and join us" the man continued and the grin widened, threatening to split his face in two. "Unlock the door and become one with the chaos."

To their surprise, Adam moved closer. It was as if part of his body, unwittingly, dragged him towards the doors, part of him trying to fight it. His fingertips slid up the glass, towards the lock. The grinning face moving up and down as digits inched towards the steel knob. Before Adam had reached the lock Emma had sprung from Sanna, grabbed him by his hoodie, and yanked him back onto the hard floor. The man behind the glass screamed with such intensity that Sanna thought the glass must surely shatter. Adam shook his head and looked at his own hand in disbelief.

"Turn on the lights" he shouted and Sanna leaped to flick a switch on the wall.

Suddenly, the corridor erupted in white fluorescent brilliance, flickering a couple of times as if threatening to die. Sanna blinked to adjust her eyes to the invasive brightness of artificial daylight. She heard another scream from the entrance. This time it was much different. The previous one had been a cry of disappointment, this one sounded like agony, pain interpreted by human vocal cords. She saw the figure at the door shy away from the brightness. His brow smoking and blistering violently. Teeth bared with an expression of excruciating anguish. Emma and Adam scooted backward towards her as the quills returned to tap on the glass, first in a disorganized fashion only to fall in time with each other once again.

They moved into the library to assess the situation. It was far enough from the entrance so the tapping was inaudible and they deemed it safer. It was possible to see others coming for them since the walls were all glass. They needed to catch their breaths and try to understand what was happening.

"So what was that?" Emma asked Adam, who was spread out across a couple of tables in the heart of the library. "Do you even know?"

Adam raised his head to look at her as she sat down on one of the puff stools that placed there for comfort. "I don't know what those fuckers are" he retorted. "They all of a sudden showed up."

"But you've been out there," Sanna said leaning against one of the bookcases. "You definitely know more than we do."

"That's true" Adam sat up. "Look. All I know is that those things are everywhere. Charlie, Mel, Julie, some others and I were hanging over by Powder Hill when this green gas stuff started spraying from over by the lake. It almost looked like one of those nuclear explosions and then smoke just kind of came from there. The earth started shaking."

"There was an earthquake?" Sanna stiffened.

"Yes, but that was later" he answered. "First we just stuck around and tried to call different folks to see if they knew what was going on, but there was no reception so we just waited. Charlie told me he heard something in the woods around the parking lot, but we just told him he was a pussy. Then the lights around us all went out and those things came out from the woods."

"You mean those men and women behind you?" Emma was visibly shaking now.

"Yes, but they weren't all sweaty and stuff then. They looked pretty normal, just those fucking smiles on their faces and glowing eyes. They carried sharp sticks, dragging them behind and started talking a bunch of gibberish about us joining them" he became agitated as he spoke. "Mel and Charlie walked over to them to try to chase them away. Charlie was convinced they were some kind of bums from across the lake, but they looked so nicely dressed to me, suits and shit. So Mel and Chuck tried to scare them off when Mel says that one of them is Mr. Birch, the biology teacher, and before they can do anything else, one of them stabs Charlie right through with the stick. Like right through. Blood just poured out of him. Chuck tried to run, but they grabbed him and pulled him away. Some of the others ran to help, but they were overpowered. I saw Pete Rollins slam one of them in the head with a tire iron, but the guy just spit out his teeth and smiled."

"That sounds kind of unbelievable" Sanna had lost interest in his story and had started flipping through a book titled *The Wisconsin* by an August Derleth someone had left on the table.

"That is true" Emma continued and looked at them both. "If they were so powerful how come you are here and what happened to everyone else."

"Are you guys fucking kidding me?" Adam rose from the tables. "Didn't you see those things? They're sensitive to light. It's what makes them sweat and their skin melt. That is why they moved when you turned on the lights. Otherwise, they would have entered. The street lights and the spots at the entrance are too weak to have any effect other than slow burning."

"How do you know that?" Sanna was beginning to think it was all an elaborate hoax to get to her.

"When Chuck went down Julie jumped into her car and the headlights made them scream and move. She turned on the high beams as soon as she understood what had happened, she was so smart."

Emma shuddered as he referred to her in the past tense. It could only mean one thing. As if on cue, there was a loud explosion outside in the parking lot and they ran over to a window.

The parking lot was in darkness. Apart from the car on fire, crashed into what must have been an electrical center. Figures stood in a semicircle around the burning vehicle. They were completely still, their shadows cast out on the wet asphalt. Limbs impossibly stretched out like a gathering of slendermen leaning towards them. Suddenly the door to the demolished car opened, and a figure stepped out, body completely engulfed in flames. Emma was certain that she should have heard the person scream in agony, even at this distance, through the window and walls. All she could do was watch as the person stumbled from side to side, walking into the others watching it as it burned. It collapsed to its knees and then sagged to kiss the damp ground.

"Get away from there" Adam cried and yanked them back by their arms, just in time for Emma to see the things turn around to look straight at them.

"Are you guys nuts?" Adam screamed at them. "Now that they have shut off all the lights out there they can probably move freely and we're sitting ducks. They are going to try to find a way inside."

"So they're smart?" Emma asked.

"Obviously. They can drive cars and speak." Adam slumped down in one of the beanbag chairs.

They remained around the table in silence for a long while; hours passed as they paced the floor, sometimes peering out the window to see what the figures outside were up to.

"They probably retain most of their normal faculties" Sanna finally broke the silence. "They don't seem to be zombies at all, which is what I thought they were from the beginning, because of the skin thing. They can express themselves; they can solve problems, which we witnessed. Therefore, it is likely that whatever they could do before they changed, if that is what we call it, they still have the ability to do."

"There are more than those guys" Adam interjected, ignoring the daggers Sanna shot at him. "When I drove over here I saw a bunch of them attacking people. Stabbing them with those sticks."

Do we assume that those they don't kill they turn?" Emma asked.

"Maybe. I didn't stick around to see what happened to Chuck or the others, but all the crazies must be coming from somewhere, plus I saw a bunch of people I recognized out there."

"Are you saying that our families might be turned?" Emma just realized the implications of what she was saying. "Or are being hurt by them."

"My mom's out there, and my little sister" Adam shouted.

"Shhh" Sanna put out her hand to make Adam stop his ranting. "Did you hear that?"

There was a sound coming from somewhere among the shelved books. A melody, someone whistling.

Adam crouched down and moved towards the nearest shelf. The whistling stopped dead and Adam tilted his head to the side waiting for some other noise to follow. There was a pregnant pause apart from the gentle hum from air vents and a blinking fluorescent light in the distance. The person began walking again, coming closer. Adam made ready to pounce as the steps closed in on their position.

Too many teeth for their mouths, Sanna thought to herself. *Can't whistle.* Before she could stop him, Adam attacked the man coming out from behind the shelves, smacking him across the head with a large tome he had picked up.

The man fell to the floor, clutching the back of his head as Adam straddled him, getting ready to pummel again.

"Wait" Sanna cried. "Stop it, it's a person."

Adam stopped and climbed off the body as the man slowly turned and cursed at them. It was the school librarian Nick. His portly figure dressed in striped pajamas and sporting toothpaste around his mouth.

"What the hell are you doing?" he said, his hand tangled in the mop of black hair on his head, rubbing the place he had been struck.

"Sorry, bro," Adam said and dropped the book. "We thought you were one of the creepies."

"One of the what?" Nick tried to get up, but his frame made it difficult and both Emma and Sanna ran over to assist him.

"Where have you been?" Sanna asked him as he sat down in a chair. "The world is going crazy out there, people are dying and ghouls are everywhere."

Nick frowned and shook his head. "I've been in here all day. Haven't noticed a thing."

"You mean to tell us you didn't even notice the earth shake before?" Emma said in disbelief.

"Not really. I was in the cafeteria to get something to eat and then got ready for bed. What do you mean people are dying?"

"Bro," Adam began. "It's complete chaos out there. These creatures are killing everyone, the lake is on fire or something, and the world is going under." It was if he was looking for the only adult in the room to come give an explanation.

"Come on guys" Nick chuckled. "You can't be serious. You're starting to sound like those other kids, your friends in fact," he pointed to Emma and Sanna. "Looking for answers to weird phenomena that are all easily explained. I'm sure it's just a flash mob or something."

"Flash mob?" Emma wrinkled her nose at the suggestion.

"If you don't believe us then why don't you look out that window and tell us what you see?" Adam suggested.

"Fine" Nick said scornfully. "You going to make me get up after you mauled me with the Necronomicon?"

"Dude, I don't even know what that means" Adam replied.

Nick looked at the trio and slowly walked over to the window; not completely convinced they were lying to him. He stared out over the dark parking lot, the car still quite visibly ablaze. He remained there a few minutes before turning back to them.

"All I see is a car on fire, having crashed into an electrical box and some weird lights in the sky with smoke rising from the city. I am sure it is all some kind of natural phenomenon making people a bit crazy. It happens all the time, why in..." before he could finish his history lecture, the window shattered and a large quill grazed his arm.

Nick spun around clutching the cut and squealed falling to the floor again. Through the broken glass stepped two of the ghoulish figures, a man and a woman. Sanna recognized them as attendants at the local gas station, because of their uniforms. As soon as they came in the bright light of the library they gritted their teeth through and their skin began to pop, sizzle and blister. The man grabbed the quill and the woman collapsed to her knees, the light being too much for her.

Sanna saw that she had a big gash in her gut, blood staining the light blue shirt and drops of crimson trickling down. Nick tried to crawl away from them but was having difficulties getting up on the slick stone floor. Adam was hesitantly moving towards him with his arm outstretched, but the man, now unsteadily clutching the stick stared straight at him as he drove the point through Nick's back with such force, breaking it in half.

Nick screamed and the woman howled as she flung herself at Adam, who sidestepped and punched her in the face. They heard a wet sound as fist met oozing skin. She flew into the wall and lay still, leaving a wet stain where she had hit. The man yanked what was left of the stick from Nick's body.

The librarian was not moving, floating in a pool of his own blood like an iceberg bobbing in the arctic sea. The man wobbled back and forth, seemingly trying to get his bearings. Adam took his chance and tackled him. Driving the figure back towards the window. Adam shrieked, the man cried out in anger, arms flailing in a vain attempt at stabbing the youngster with the remaining stick. His back cracked against the window frame and Adam backed off, letting the body collapse.

The man slid down, the back of his head impaled on a shard of glass. His momentum coming to an abrupt halt. The glow in his eyes slowly faded as he hanged from his skull. Instantly his skin started to change. It looked like a transparent balloon filled with muddy water. Veins closest to the surface fully visible, bones and teeth floating around inside. There was a small pop as one of the blisters exploded and murky liquid ran from the hole, emptying the sack that had once been a person. Adam stepped back and looked over at the woman's body. Nothing remained of her, just a gas station uniform in a puddle of bodily fluids among bits of bones and cartilage.

"What the fuck is going on?" Adam screamed.

"Is he alive?" Emma whispered. Still on the floor, quickly covered in human remains.

"I think he's dead," Adam said as he tried to lean over the body without getting gore on his shoes. "I can't see him breathing at all and there is nothing we can do for him without a doctor. He's lost too much blood." He was strangely calm after having killed two people and seen a third die, Sanna observed.

"We could go to the school nurse's office and see what she has," Emma suggested.

"Dude, he's dead or dying" Adam retorted. "What the fuck would we be able to do for him? He needs a fucking hospital, not a god damn Tylenol."

"We need to get out of this room" Sanna had just realized their situation. "If those two could get in here, then there must be a fire escape, drainpipe, or something they climbed up on. There are more of them out there and we are close enough to the window for them to attempt it."

"So where do we go?" Adam snorted at the idea.

"The further into the building we go, the more difficult it must be for those things to reach us. They seem to suffer from the light quite quickly. So, the longer they have to move through it the worse for them and safer for us." Emma rose from the floor.

"What about Nick?" Sanna whispered.

"Like Adam said, I think he's beyond what we can do for him." Tears welled in Emma's eyes. "We have to look out for ourselves now."

Adam pulled one of the library shelves over to cover the broken window, just to be on the safe side, and then they moved to the center of the school. Still shaken from the incident, they tried to have a coherent conversation about where would be the safest place to hide out. In the end, they all agreed that if the objective were to last the night, in the hopes that natural sunlight might kill off the ghouls or at least force them into hiding then the school cafeteria would be their best bet. Once daybreak had arrived, they would clear out of the building and head to wherever.

As they walked down the winding corridors, Adam repeatedly tried to contact his mother by phone, but like Sanna, he had no luck. The lack of success seemed to make him more and more agitated still he kept trying. Hoping that someone might eventually answer.

"So you never told us how you managed to get away from the ghouls in the first place" Sanna attempting distraction.

"What?" Adam bit off at first but calmed down. "From Powder Hill?"

"Yeah" Sanna was relieved to see his change in demeanor. *So much rage in there*, she thought. *Must avoid him directing it at us.*

"I think you were telling us that you and Julie got in the car," she continued in a soothing voice.

"Julie was in the car with the headlights on, but she was scared shitless" Adam began. His eyes darting this way and that, peeking around corners to avoid any ambush. "I had to push her to the passenger seat so we could get away, but they followed us."

He paused for a moment. Emma and Sanna remained silent, waiting for the next part. Instead, Adam turned to them with a smile.

"We have arrived ladies," he said instead.

The school cafeteria was located in the heart of the building, devoid of windows. Adam slowly opened one of the great double doors and looked around. He was unarmed so Sanna wondered what his plan was if he were to encounter something on the other side, but it was all clear.

They walked into the wide-open space so typical of your garden-variety lunchroom. All tiles, white plastic tables with attached seats, made for easy cleaning and buffet carts standing in neat little rows separating students from the lunch ladies. An unmistakable odor of grease hung in the air like a ghost of meals past.

"This seems cozy enough" Emma attempted to smile sarcastically.

"There might be some food in the pantry or walk-in that we can take," Adam said as he headed to the back room. "I, for one, am starving."

He took a few steps into the kitchen area when the lights flickered. Once, twice and then died completely, leaving them in utter darkness.

Emma let out a yelp while trying to locate Sanna, who had frozen in place. Adam ran over to the doors and looked down the empty hallways. The translucent emergency tape running along the floor was the only thing glowing. He turned back around, the reflective light hinting at his shape.

"Shit," he said to himself. "Everyone, just stand still for a moment."

"What happened?" Sanna said desperately.

"Well, obviously those things found the main fuse box," Adam replied.

"What do we do now?" Sanna continued and stretched out her arms in an attempt at finding something familiar.

"What can we do?" Emma sobbed quietly to herself. She had found one of the benches and sprawled out over it, trying to make sense of it all.

"We're sitting ducks in here once they find their way inside. That's one thing that's certain." Adam replied. "I think our advantage of sitting here is that it will be a while until they find us."

"Yes, but once they do we have nowhere to run." Emma clasped her clammy hands to her damp forehead.

"That's not completely true," Sanna said. "We can escape through the kitchen. There is an exit next to the loading dock back there."

"Then why don't we leave now?" They could hear Adam's footsteps move in what they thought was the direction of the kitchen as he spoke."

"Because we don't know if any of them are outside waiting for us," Sanna retorted. "They are most likely walking around the building waiting for us to come out, or to get in. If we wait in here, we at least have a chance at hearing them break in and then probably several hours before they find us. By then we can high tail it out of here."

"That sounds good to me" Emma sighed. "Nothing like just waiting to die:"

"What do you suggest we do then?" Sanna found that talking to each other in the dark was quite nice; she could avoid paying attention to facial cues.

"I didn't say I had any other plan" Emma shot back. "We can't fight them so we might as well hold up here in hopes that daybreak is on its way." She could see the faint glow from Sanna's cell phone in the dark. "What time is it?"

"It's close to three a.m." Sanna replied in a despondent tone.

"So we have about three hours or so before dawn breaks" Adam cut in. "If we're lucky they won't find us in a few hours. I say we wait here and get some rest. One of us can keep watch while the others snooze. So that we are fresh once we need to run."

That will never work Emma thought. It was more likely that they would be groggy in the dark and fall over things if woken from a dead sleep, but she had stopped caring at this point. If she was going to die at the hands of hellish ghouls from the other side then so mote it be. What worried her was the whereabouts of her parents. Were they looking for her, out there braving the chaos? Her dad would fight tooth and nail to get to her if he believed she was still alive. Her chest ached as she wished that she were half as brave. That she dared walk out that door in the kitchen and battle what might be on the other side in order to find her loved ones or just to know what had befallen them. She sighed again and covered her eyes with her arm.

"I'll take the first watch," Adam said in a tone that begged them to praise his manliness. "Save your cell phone batteries for the torches later."

Rest did not come easy. Sanna had settled by the kitchen entrance in order to get a better vantage point from which to run. Emma had declined an invitation to join her, citing that she was quite comfortable. In fact, Emma felt she needed a break. It was what always happened between them. They were the best of friends most days, but they both had quirks that in small doses were endearing, but quickly became annoying.

Adam moved a bench in front of the double doors separating them from the corridor. It made a horrendous noise as he dragged it. Emma stared up at the dark ceiling waiting to hear the sounds of footsteps coming towards them. She tried to focus on the darkness and just as she figured she would never find sleep, her eyelids became heavy.

Sanna rested her head on the cool counter, hoping that some of the chill would refrigerate her searing brain. Her mind was racing. She had not processed everything that had happened since she had looked up from that microscope. A myriad of what-ifs buzzed around inside her. What if they'd gone home? Had she died with her mother and brother then? In their house? Her thoughts paused at the image of her family, but she quickly swatted them away. Was it worth imagining what was going to happen next? If they survive the night, was there anything on the other side of this purgatory. Was she all alone in the world? Could she handle that? The line between the dark of the room and the dark of sleep became blurred and she lost herself in a state of semi-sleep.

A loud crash somewhere in the distance interrupted their dreams. They jerked awake. The torch from Adam's phone lit his face, eyes darting back and forth.

"What the hell was that?" He said in a muddled state.

"They're here," Sanna whispered.

"Where did it come from?" Emma asked as she sat up. "She was trying to keep panic from her voice.

"It might have been the main entrance" Adam had scooted his body closer to the doors, listening intently. Both Sanna and Emma had tiptoed towards him. "It doesn't seem as if they're headed this way." Adam continued. "They're probably going room by room and, depending on how many they are, they won't find us for a while."

"As long as we don't make a sound," Sanna added. The other two turned to stare at her in the white glow of cellular illumination. "What?" She replied to them in a loud whisper. "Don't you worry about me; I know how to shut up."

"We need to get out of here" Adam exclaimed. "They will be here sooner than later."

"We can't be sure that the back entrance is safe" Emma interjected. "If we open those doors and the back lot is filled with them then we are screwed for sure."

"We can take a look carefully and then if we see something we can sneak back," Adam said as he moved away from the doors.

"We can't take that chance" Emma was trying not to raise her voice. "For all we know, they're waiting for us."

****

"That could be no matter when we make our move" there was irritation in his voice. "I need to get out of here. I need to know if my mom and baby sister are still alive."

"The longer we hold out, the better chance we have of survival," Emma pleaded.

"The longer we wait here, the more likely it is that they have been killed. I've been sitting here too long already. I wasn't supposed to be here. I was going straight home no matter what she said, and then I ended up here anyway."

"Who said?" Emma felt a tinge of worry in her chest."

"It doesn't matter" Adam brushed her off. "I need to give it a try no matter what." They could hear the sound of doors kicked in far off down the corridors beyond their hiding place.

He moved further away, but Emma grabbed his sleeve. "Don't" she said with a tremble in her voice. "You'll kill us all."

"Look, you can come with me and maybe we'll survive, or you remain here and you won't. The choice is yours."

This is the point of no return... Sanna gently sang in her mind. The only coherent thing inside there as the crashing of wood and glass came closer, followed by whoops and guttural shouts from hoarse throats.

Adam walked into the kitchen and headed for the loading dock. The girls looked at each other and then followed him. Not because Sanna needed protection from a man, but she might be able to push him in front of her if ambushed.

The kitchen was even eerier than the cafeteria had been. She was uncomfortable around inanimate and unused objects. She could accept being in the kitchen when it was bustling with activity, but like this; all dark and desolate, with pots and pans just sitting there, the dishwasher open and silent. It was like a ghost town complete with the ghosts of lunch ladies past dancing among the appliances and utensils.

Once they had reached the doors, Adam handed Emma his phone so that he could use both hands to gingerly, putting his shoulder into it, open the metal door. Sanna expected it to creak noisily, but it was silent. She relaxed. Adam peered out the tiny crack he had created and then indicated that he saw nothing. Therefore, he pushed it a bit more. The glow of night cut through the dark. There was noise out there. The cries of people echoing across the town, the red glow of fires, and a low rumbling as the billowing clouds continued to roll across the sky.

"There are five of them standing in the parking lot, looking over here," Adam whispered.

"Have they seen you?" Emma replied.

"Not yet but we can't go this way. It's too risky."

Just as he whispered those last words, someone tried to open the entrance to the cafeteria. First, it was a gentle push, the door catching against the bench. Then there was another attempt, firmer this time and with more authority. Finally, there was a loud crash as a body or bodies barreled into the obstacle. The crash and shriek of metal against tile caused Emma to let out a scream before she could cover her mouth. There was silence for what seemed like an eternity, as if the creatures on the other side were assessing if they had truly heard something. Sanna grabbed Emma's clammy hand as the ghouls heaved against the doors again.

"Run!" Adam shouted, kicking the door wide open and ducking outside. The girls followed, not knowing quite what to expect. Sanna paused as the cool night air touched her skin and she felt as if she could breathe clean air instead of recycled desperation from fellow students. They stood still on the raised platform where deliveries arrived. A chill ran up and down Sanna's spine, tears welled in Emma's eyes and Adam clenched his fists.

"Shit," he said as ghouls still standing around the wreckage of a now smoldering car, saw them and started running, spear-like sticks raised above their heads.

"There," Emma screamed, pointing at the fire escape. "We can climb to the roof."

Adam bounded up the iron ladder, taking the rungs two at time. Emma and Sanna close behind, but less speedily. As soon as Sanna's feet had left the platform, she clearly heard the door to the cafeteria fly open. She hurried as the whoops and screams from hellish ghouls came from all directions in a raucous onslaught. She looked up and saw Adam pushing against the side rails. A vein bulging at his temple as he exerted his energy without result.

"What the hell are you doing?" Emma yelled and pushed him back across the rooftop with one hand.

"Nothing" Adam looked indignant. "Trying to help you guys by keeping the ladder steady."

"Fuck you" Emma shot back as Sanna put her feet down on the concrete floor. "You were trying to push us down."

"Yes, ok I was trying to push you down" his eyes went dark and the familiar sound of shoes upon metal could clearly be heard as the ladder vibrated with the weight of bodies. "Can you blame me for wanting to get rid of dead weight?"

"You're fucking dead weight," Emma cried and closed in on him.

Suddenly Sanna saw Emma's head jerk to the side and her body roll off to the side. Adam's arm extended, fist balled. Sanna ran towards her friend on the ground. Blood trickled from her nose and mouth where Adam's fist had landed.

"What are you doing?" Sanna cried at him while cradling her friend's head in her arms. Adam was breathing heavily, slightly hunched over like a predatory animal about to pounce.

"Oh, nothing much," he said through gritted teeth. "Just making sure those things have something to do while I make my escape."

"Why?"

"I need to get to my mom and sister," he said as he slowly dug something out of his pocket. "I need to save them."

"You don't even know if they're still alive."

"Maybe they are" in his hands was the point of the quill that had killed Nick. Adam quickly grabbed her arm and yanked her away from Emma. "I need you too."

"Let go of me" she tried to claw at his eyes, but he was too strong, and she felt like a rag doll in his tight grip.

"She can occupy the ones on the ladder while you will work as a toy for the ones in the parking lot." He rested the point tightly under her chin as he pulled her to the opposite end of the roof. Sanna cried for Emma, who was stirring on the ground.

Pushing her head over the edge, they could both clearly see a truck parked close to the building. Surrounding it were the ghouls, sticks pointing at them, their eyes aglow, and their menacing grins.

"We will jump onto the back of that delivery truck and then I will push you off to those things and then I will be free to run away."

"You'll never make it" she stuttered.

"I will never know if I don't try." He pushed the point deeper to cement his decision. "It worked before."

"You killed Julie?" Her eyes went wide with the realization.

"She wanted to head out of town when I told her I needed to get home. So I pushed her, as simple as that."

"Adam" came a voice from the ladder. They both looked over to where it came from. The head peering over the edge had once belonged to their classmate Julie. Her eyes were different and on her face was a wide vicious grin and her once beautiful blond hair lay plastered against a skull that sported a deep gash from the left temple to the jaw. "Did you miss me?" She continued.

Adam's jaw fell open and Sanna saw her opportunity. With as much force as she could muster, she rammed her elbow into his ribs. Adam coughed and let go. Emma, who had now regained her faculties, ran towards them, but he recovered quickly and with one simple pushed sent Sanna toppling over the edge. There was a sick thud as Emma heard her hit the truck. She continued to move at him, but he tackled her to the ground, knocking the wind out of her. He rose and paused momentarily. It was the opening she needed and kicked him hard in the shin, managing to sweep both legs from underneath him. He fell hard and she rolled onto her stomach in time to see Julie climb up.

Adam was up again and swung the spear point at her. Without thinking, she dodged making him go wide and off-center. With all her might, she barreled into him. In an uncontrollable mass of flailing limbs, they both rammed Julie, whose grip on the sides of the ladder was so tight that Adam's body on her caused the bolts, weakened from his earlier attempt at loosening them, to let go. Emma fell back as she watched the two of them careen towards the wet ground. Adam cried out as Julie dug her manicured nails into his flesh followed by the sound of bodies hitting asphalt.

****

Emma quickly ran to the other end and looked down. Sanna was writhing on the roof of the trailer. She had created a dent, bit apart from general pain she seemed to be fine. The ghouls surrounding the truck were banging on its sides in an obvious attempt to scare her.

"I'll be right down" she cried to her friend. Still fueled by the adrenaline that had given her the fortitude to kill a man she had no qualms about leaping off a building. She climbed the little ledge and flung herself, not even considering how she was going to land. She crashed hard on her side instead of landing on her feet and rolling. Part of her landed on Sanna's legs hurting her even more. Emma collapsed next to her friend, panting heavily.

"What happened to Adam?" Sanna asked wearily.

"He won't bother us anymore" Emma replied and smiled, blood running into her mouth.

"Dawn is coming" Sanna turned her head towards the east and a small sliver of gold was visible. As she said it with hope in her voice, the semi-trailer started shaking and they could hear the sound of feet and hands against metal.

They both turned around and looked up to see ghouls climbing up the engine compartment. They were slow and deliberate, trapping them.

Emma sat up. They had come so far and overcome so much. Now they would die all the same.

"Emma" Sanna said and looked her in the eyes, holding her head in the palms of her hands. "Listen to me."

"What?" Emma sobbed.

"You have to run."

"What are you talking about?"

"Only one of us can survive this," Sanna continued. "I want it; no I need it to be you."

"No, I can't."

"I can distract them, and you can get away. You can have a chance if you run and don't stop until the sun comes up. Maybe you can find your family or our friends or just get out of here, but you have to go."

"I can't. You mustn't sacrifice yourself for me. It's not worth it."

"It's not worth us both dying. Whatever happens after tonight the world isn't a world I can live in. I have enough troubles living in the normal world, but at least I knew how things worked. I had my routines, my family, but they might not be around. The world I had neatly arranged is no more. How am I supposed to live now? I can't start over."

"But you can live with me" Emma tried.

"No, that's not how it works for me. You know that." Sanna kissed her on the forehead and then rose. She stared at her, ghouls having reached the cabin, stretched out her arms. "Emma?"

"Yes, Sanna." Emma reached for her friend.

"Run!" Sanna screamed as she fell backward. Emma cried as her friend tumbled off the trailer and took the ghouls with her as she fell. They slid like a boulder off the truck. Emma, in somewhat of a state of shock, wiped her face and then followed, sliding off the engine and down to the ground. Ghouls, who were not clutching Sanna, grabbed for her, but she untangled herself and ran. She headed east, towards the sun. She glanced over her shoulder and caught a glimpse of Sanna in a mass of creatures and she caught her eye. Those wet blue eyes staring at her, urging her on.

****

There was no time for tears. She continued to run. Her lungs burning, her mouth dry, her eyes watering. Her entire body was in pain. Out of the parking lot, past cars and buildings on fire and bodies strewn about. Until she reached Washington where she halted for a moment.

The sun was rising above the billowing clouds over Pike Lake, bathing the world in golden light. She thought she could hear the sound of sirens off in the distance. Maybe someone in a neighboring town had seen the fires and contacted the authorities. She tried to stay in the sun. That was where she felt safe for the moment.

The adrenaline left her body and her legs could no longer carry her weight. She collapsed in the middle of the street. Looked towards the high school and wept.

Postman from the Other Side
By Shashi Kadapa

In Dharwad of 190's India, black magic swayed rural areas. A headless postman from the 1880s seeks restitution and bliss for his soul.

As the cyclist came abreast, a bolt of lightning lit up the night and Gopi could briefly see the apparition. With a start, he realized that a gaping black hole yawned, with blood and gore where there should have been a head. The lightning struck again, and Gopi felt a rush of fear as he saw the blackness between the collar and the bleeding hands stripped of skin that gripped the handlebars, with bulging veins, pulsating, and squirting blood...

Chapter 1
The Beginning

My name is Shiva. I am a teller of tales of rural India. This story begins a few months back when I went to buy some postage stamps in the hamlet Hooli, about 50 kilometers from Dharwad town. Hooli has several temples, built hundreds of years ago, and is reputed for black magic, exorcism, and Māṭagāti or witches. Residents do not venture alone out of their homes after sunset. The common refrain is that many black magic rituals have left unsatiated spirits prowling the countryside, seeking to devour helpless souls and bodies.

On my earlier visits to Hooli, I had seen this old man Krishna, a retired postman, as he sat on the bench in the verandah of the local post office, mumbling and dozing. His hands were gnarled like the trunk of the Banyan tree, the veins digging out from his wasted skin like fat and distended earthworms. His frail body huddled in the old khaki dress of the postman of a bygone era, a shock of thin straggly white hair peeped out from his cap.

The village elders recalled seeing him since their childhood and he seemed like a sentinel, watching and waiting, just like the mute ancient temples in the loping countryside. As he rode an old creaky cycle around the village, with a small brown satchel hung from his bicycle carrier, probably a relic of old times, he seemed to be one with the decrepit temples in the village. I thought he was sure to be a treasure trove of ancient tales and I tried goading him to make him speak.

"This town is only for pensioners who probably lead a life of no interest. Pity the dam did not drown this village."

He sat quiet and uncaring, probably listening to some memories.

I taunted him "This is a dead town, nothing has ever happened here."

This elicited some reaction. He looked at me with old rheumy eyes that suddenly turned opaque and then almost normal. His voice came in rasps from his bony chest. It was like listening to a hollow voice emanating from a deep well.

"I have seen and heard things that would make you tremble like a leaf.", he said.

I was eager to listen. "So go ahead, old man. Scare me."

With trembling hands, the old man asked me to bring him his old satchel tied to the cycle. He placed it on his lap and told his story. The next pages are his words. I am but the narrator. The story begins during the British rule in India in the early 1900s.

Chapter 2
The First Encounter

The rain-bearing winds of the monsoon shrieked through the dusk, and the first large raindrops spattered on the new postman Gopi Kulkarni as he furiously pedaled through a narrow tree-lined path. Bolts of lightning shattered the darkness, filling the evening with bright flashes that showed a long winding path with bends.

Gopi was energetic, outgoing, liked to socialize, mix with people, and listen to them, and he was honorable. His work as a postman brought him into contact with the villagers, most of who were illiterate. He read their mail to them, wrote responses, listened to their troubles, and advised them. People would wait for him, charmed by his lively personality and they trusted him.

He would soon come to the stone bridge that straddled a small canal through which water flowed to the dam. The water had turned brown with the silt that it carried from the hills. Branches and forest debris floated and bobbed in the current.

The stone bridge was a few spans long and broad enough for a bullock cart to pass. Built many decades back, the road was cobbled making drivers jerk sharply as they went over it. A sharp slope led from the path to the bridge and Gopi would stop pedaling when he reached the decline, coasting down the bridge and then picking up the pace strenuously as he rode up the incline to his home.

Gopi was gasping with the effort as he steadied himself just as the heavens opened up, bringing down a deluge.

Muddy waters sloshed across the bridge and approaching cautiously, he squinted through the heavy downpour and started on the downward slope. He was midway down the path when he realized that another cyclist was coming up.

'*Probably a villager from the neighboring village.*' he thought.

He shifted his attention to the road carefully guiding his cycle between potholes and ruts, taking care to avoid sharp stones. The other cyclist was near enough for Gopi to see that he was wearing the Khaki uniform of a postman.

'*Strange*', he thought '*there are just two postmen in the office, himself and a colleague. His friend had finished the delivery and was safe in his home. So, where was this fellow from?*'

As the cyclist came abreast, a bolt of lightning lit up the night. *With a start, Gopi realized that he could only see a black hole where there should have been the man's face.*

The light was gone in an instant and Gopi later recalled the rush of adrenalin that gripped him as he saw the apparition, with skeletal hands gripping the handlebars of the cycle tightly.

Gopi was in a frenzy as he controlled his cycle over the rough cobblestones. The figure seemed to have disappeared in the rain. He thought *bah, darkness and lightning are playing tricks on my mind. Imagine! A rider without a head. Yes, my wife, Lata, will find this funny.*

Gopi rode into his gate, soaking wet, and smiled at his wife Lata who cradled their baby. The gate was made of small wooden frames bolted into two poles that stood in the thick bushes that made the hedge. Laughing at the chortling baby, he wiped the rain off himself as best as he could and picked up the tot. He loved his family, they were everything to him.

"Lata. You will not believe it. Something funny happened when I was riding back."

His wife was busy preparing tea and dinner. She looked her shoulder as Gopi played with the baby.

"What happened?"

"I was riding back home and though I saw another postman cross me on the bridge. I looked at him and saw that he did not have a head.

Then he started laughing at the incident. The baby also joined, gurgling with his father.

Lata frowned "Without a head? Must be the rain. You did not see him properly? Perhaps there was no rider, and you saw your own shadow."

The encounter was forgotten as Gopi played with his gurgling baby. Lata lit another kerosene lamp and he gossiped with his wife and told her about his colleagues and office politics, local gossip and petty jealousies and rivalries that are a part of any community.

With the baby asleep, they made love passionately and snuggled, cozy in their warm embrace. Late in the night, Gopi woke to a small hammering sound that seemed to come from outside. *'Must be the wind banging the loose gate.'*

Dawn breaks early in the countryside. Gopi was up and drinking a cup of tea as he gazed out of the window. It had rained heavily the previous night and water ran everywhere in tiny streams.

Then he saw something brown buried in the ground outside the window. He got up and saw a khaki sack used by postmen to deliver mail. Red liquid was oozing from the sack and made thin trails in the water. Just then, his wife shouted that hot water was ready for his bath. He went in and forgot about the sack. Preoccupied with his pending work at the office, he did not even glance at the area outside his window.

At the post office, he got swept up with work and soon forgot about the cyclist he had met the previous evening. As the other postmen returned to the office in the evening he remembered the apparition he had met the previous evening. There were four staff members, he and another postman Balu, Appa the mail sorter, and Pandhari who handled money orders.

He casually remarked "I saw another postman yesterday. In the heavy rain, I could not see him clearly, and he appeared to be headless."

The next instant, there was pin-drop silence!

The staff stared at him with horror and they shuffled out silently. They stood in the verandah and stood jabbering, looking at Gopi with fear.

Slightly perturbed, Gopi asked "What is the problem? Why are you muttering among yourselves? You know anything?"

The staff shuffled their feet and looked around furtively, giving no explanation. Gopi shrugged helplessly. He *would not get any answer from them. They would talk later when things had cooled down.*

Chapter 3
The Second Encounter

Distributing salaries to the staff at the Post Office was one of Gopi's jobs. He picked up the employee register, which had information on salaries paid, leave taken, and other details going back a few decades. When he did not have much to do, Gopi often browsed through the pages, and read the notations of his colleagues long ago.

As he turned the pages he noticed that one page was torn and only the top half remained. An entry was barely visible. It was the last salary paid to one Gopal Rao, employee number 971. Where there should have been a signature was only a thumb impression.

This disturbed him. As a rule, only literate postmen were hired. Whose thumb impression could this be?

Scrawled in small, barely legible writing, he made out the words 'wife of deceased.' Gopi showed the torn page to Appa and other staff.

"Who tore off this page? This is an offense."

The staff stared fearfully at the torn page and shook their heads.

Appa the mail sorter and the senior-most staff member walked over. "Look at the date. It is 15 January 1880, more than 70 years back. How will we who tore off the page? "

With a snort of disgust, Gopi put the register down and returned to his work.

With all mail and money orders delivered and rain threatening to pour down in buckets he decided to go home early. He bought some groceries and was soon off. His thoughts wandered to his family and his job. *I love the job, my nice cottage with a garden, a loving wife, and a baby. The work is not strenuous; the villagers respect me because I am one of the few literate people in the village. Plus, there is a pension after I retire.*

Shortly he approached the tree-lined path. The branches, heavy with water had bunched and closed to form a canopy along the path. Diffused light wafted through dimly, covering small patches in darkness.

Gopi suddenly realized that he had company. He looked back to see another cyclist coming up fast behind him. *Good. A bit of company would be nice.*

Gopi liked to make friends and he wanted to spend a few minutes speaking with the rider. Strangers showed respect when they came to know that he was a postman, and he liked to be respected. The cyclist was now just a few paces behind him and he could hear furious pedaling.

He sneaked a look behind as he slowed down to let the other fellow catch up. From the corner of his eye, he saw a bicycle wheel come into his view; the handlebars dimly glinting in the dark. A pair of khaki-clad pants pedaled hard. Gopi jerked his eyes at the dark road ahead as he stumbled into a pothole, regained balance, and then glanced sideways again.

Skeletal hands with the flesh partially stripped away held the handlebars in a tight grip, finger bones with loose flesh stretched tightly. Worn sandals pushed the pedals in jerks, not in the smooth motion of a cyclist. The veins and tendons stood out starkly, pulsating and throbbing, with blood squirting out. The arms led to a neck and then.. nothing! Utter panic filled his stomach, as he realized that there was no head.

The apparition raised its hand to try to catch him. Gopi's first reaction was to get down and accost the rider. However, a fear of the unknown set in. While he was composed in emergencies this unexpected sight unnerved him and he bolted, rising from the seat he shifted his weight to the handles and started pushing the pedals with all he had.

Gopi took the first bend at full speed, skidding on the gravel. The rider followed close behind, and Gopi could hear a harsh rasping sound. Then he was down the straight, pushing away and nearing the second bend. As he went into the turn, the rider shot into the inside lane and Gopi had to apply the brakes abruptly to avoid crashing into him.

Gopi was getting irritated at the tricks this fellow was playing. He reached out to catch the fellow, his cycle went into a runt, and his hands moved back to hold the handles and correct his balance.

Swerving away sharply, Gopi saw the hand waving, as if asking him to stop. The fingers were torn and the skin clung loosely from the finger bones. This was getting scary. His house was nearby and he did not want this thing to accompany him to his house.

Fighting down his disgust and with sweat pouring down his back, he pumped the pedals into a blur. Light beckoned from the edge of the canopy of branches. He felt that if he could reach the light with the apparition he could see clearly and catch the scoundrel.

The rider led him closely. His satchel cover had come loose and flopped over. The contents jerked and bounced at the motion. The next instant Gopi was in the next bend and took it sharply, going into a tight curve, with the bicycle tilting dangerously.

Gopi went faster, pumping the pedals with all he had. His front wheel was almost touching the apparition's pedals. The satchel cover of the apparition came untied and its contents glistened in the light. Gopi glanced and almost fell off as he saw the contents.

A severed neck. It was the most horrendous sight he had seen. Lightning flashed and in the brief flash, he saw blood congealed from severed arteries and the nerves, stringy and wet, hung limp and lifeless. Bloodied eyeballs rolled loose in the sockets. Skin peeled from the skull, and the mouth grimaced in a tortured cry.

He flashed through the light and was in the open. He saw a bullock cart full of people come up the road. He braked hard, skidded, and fell. Comforting hands picked him up and carried him to the cart. In a haze from the fall, he gazed back at the path instinctively. The rider had vanished.

He lay in the cart mumbling incoherently in frustrated anger about a headless cyclist. The passengers, mainly laborers who worked at the nearby dam, carried him into his house.

Gopi's wife huddled around her husband, not knowing what to do, her tense face streaked with tears. The baby sensed his mother's uneasiness and started crying. Gopi slipped into a fitful sleep.

The door slowly creaked open and the headless cyclist stood in the doorway. Rain dripped from his clothes and gathered in puddles around his legs. He held the severed head in his hands and Gopi watched unable to move, his wide-open eyes watching the figure advance into the room, beckoning him. The head opened its mouth and spoke in a harsh rasping voice 'Come, it is time'.

****

Gopi screamed loudly as he felt icy cold hands on his neck and awoke with a jerk. His wife was shaking him asking if he was all right. He wildly looked around the room shivering in his sweat-drenched clothes. The door was firmly closed, the latch drawn. There was no one; it was a nightmare. He went into a deep dreamless sleep as his wife patted his head soothingly.

He awoke in the morning with his limbs contorted in pain from the fall and stress of the previous night. He had a slight fever, a runny nose. He stretched to ease some of the stiffness as his wife walked in.

"What happened? Did something frighten you? You kept mumbling in your sleep about a headless figure. You even screamed a couple of times. Don't you remember?"

Gopi felt the words almost spilling out of him but his ego and care for his wife forced him to keep quiet. There was no point in frightening her. He stood up stiffly and beckoned a villager passing by his house. He sent a message to the post office through him saying that he was sick and would not be coming in for the day.

Chapter 4
The story of the ghost

Word of Gopi's exploits the previous evening got around fast in the small community and the local gossipmonger, the crone Gangawwa turned up. Her main pastime was to visit homes, gather information, add her bit to it, and then spread it around.

She was bent, walked with a stick and it was reputed that she was a witch. She earned her income by casting black magic spells or by removing them. No one really believed that her magic was effective. However, just to keep themselves on the right side of all spirits and not antagonize anybody they visited her hut every Saturday and bought the customary charm to ward off bad luck, a lemon strung with chilies.

After accepting a cup of tea from Lata, Gangawwa blurted out "Did the sahib really see the headless cyclist?"

Gopi still felt high strung and unsteady despite a mostly restful day. He sat up in his armchair, resentful that people refused to accept his story at face value.

"You old woman, you dare to doubt me. Anyway, what do you know about this apparition? Tell me about this ghost or whatever. What is it, why does it seek me out?'"

Gangawwa settled comfortably on the floor and asked for another cup of tea.

"Is the sahib aware that the house he lives in is built on an old shamshan graveyard?"

Seeing the stricken look on their faces, Gangavva expanded on it with relish.

"Many years ago, this area was a small private graveyard of the big landlord, The Desai. There was no road back then and there was jungle everywhere."

Pausing to sip tea she continued.

"This happened a long time ago. I was only a child then. The government acquired the land to build the dam. Surplus land was used to build government quarters. The dam swallowed the Landlord's house and the surrounding orchards. The graveyard, which sat on a hillock, was spared from being submerged. I remember the post office had just come up and people could exchange letters. All you needed was someone to read and write the postcards. There was a postman called Gopal Rao who had died horribly."

Gopal? Gopal! The name in the register, in the torn page. The half-legible name. What could possibly be the connection here?

Gopi had a vivid flashback of him hurtling through the night on his bicycle with the headless cyclist in hot pursuit. He sat up retching and coughing from the stress and the cold. Lata rushed to him to pat his forehead. Gangavva was admonished and driven out.

He went back to sleep and the morning slipped away in a daze. Late in the afternoon, Appa dropped in. He gazed intently at Gopi, seeing lines of stress on the tense face.

Gopi burst out in anger "Who was this, Gopal? Why did he die? Was this headless cyclist real?"

Raising his hands, Appa began "Gopal Rao was one of the first postmen in this area. This was a long time back, many decades ago. He would leave early, go to different houses and farms, deliver letters, read them to illiterate people, and write replies."

He paused to study the tensed Gopi and continued "The Desai, landlord or dhanyaru as he was called was cruel and usurped the land of poor farmers. He liked music and organized meets where singers and musicians were invited to perform and handsomely paid. Once Gopal Rao had to deliver a letter to the Desai. Since the landlord was illiterate, he asked Gopal to read him the letter. It was from the district magistrate and was an order to the Landlord to surrender his land for the dam. The Desai was a man of fiery temper and was a scion of the local king. Surrendering his land was like paying tribute to a conqueror, an insult, and this was unacceptable."

Appa paused to wipe his face, then resumed.

"In a fit of rage, he pulled out his sword and beheaded the postman. He then buried the headless body in the family graveyard. The head was thrown away so that the body could never be identified."

Frustrated, Gopi asked, "What has this to do with me?" Anger and outrage flooded his voice.

Appa continued " Since then, the ghost of the postman roams the countryside, searching for its head. The landlord and his family perished and drowned in the waters of the dam."

Gopi sat on the edge of the seat, his fingers locked with nervousness.

Appa continued his story "It is said that the ghost will rest in peace only if a male heir of the landlord offers the head back to the spirit. However, this is not possible since, as far as we know, the family has died out. There are rumors that one son was spirited away by a loyal servant, however, this is a rumor and the son has not appeared until now. Therefore, the headless postman roams this land forever, killing who he likes."

Angrily Gopi burst out "I do not believe this one bit. But why me? Why is this thing haunting me?"

Calmly, Appa replied "Rumor says it that the headless postman marks a person at random, takes the victim's head in the belief that it is its own head. The events will end only after an heir from the landlord's family finds the postman's head and offers it back. That will never happen since nobody knows if there are any survivors or even where they are. The apparition manifests once in a while, and horrible death has always befallen someone."

Quick to love deeply, even quicker to get angry, Gopi exploded.

"But why come after me? Will it harm my family? I swear to god, I will kill it if it even comes near my wife and kid."

Appa smiled. "Saheb, the ghost is already dead. You cannot kill it. As far as coming after you, I don't know; perhaps it wants your head."

****

Lata was very worried about her husband. *Yes, Someone's evil eye has fallen on him.*

She was very superstitious and believed in black magic Gopi however considered them as foolish. She approached Gangawwa and asked for a lucky charm amulet to be made for him.

The crone was still nursing some anger for being driven off the last time she saw Gopi. Lata enticed her with money and fruits. Somewhat mollified Gangawwa hammered out an amulet from a small brass sheet, inscribed it with symbols to ward off Shani, the god who was best worshipped to keep off bad luck. Then she made a great show of spitting on the ground around the amulet to ward off bad luck, tied it on a string, and asked Lata to make her husband wear it around the neck.

She also strung up lemons and chilies along with a small black doll to make two garlands of the stuff and asked Lata to hang them in front of the main and the rear doors of their home.

Lata said "He drives a bicycle. What about that?"

"Oh, yes. Warding off the evil eye for the cycle is very important."

She proceeded to make another garland and asked Lata to tie it on the front of the cycle.

Then she added "Take your husband to the Panchalingeshwara temple, the holy temple of Shiva. Only Shiva can remove the curse that has struck him. "

Lata nodded in assent. Gopi stoutly refused to bow to these superstitious beliefs. He said he would look foolish and face ridicule if he went around on his cycle with a lucky charm made of lemon and chilies. However, he loved his wife and cared for her physical and mental well-being. To mollify and keep his wife happy, Gopi wore it around the neck, complaining that it scratched his chest. Lata was now happy that her husband was protected.

Chapter 5
Visit to the temple

Appa and Lata prevailed on Gopi that they obtain the divine blessings of Shiva at the Panchalingeshwara temple. Built in the 11th century by the Badami Chalukya kings, the temple saw many visitors who came to pray to Shiva to remove obstacles and miseries in their life. The inner sanctum or the Garbhagruha had three shivalingas in a straight line and two on either side.

A large mukha mantapa was carved in a rectangle navaranga with five shikharas. A large entrance hall was in the form of a rectangle with five spires. The inner walls had intricate carvings depicting incidents from the Puranas and the Vedas. They showed sages, ascetics, and kings praying, performing yagnas, pujas, slaying rakshas and evil spirits. The temple was under the protection of the Archeological Survey of India, the place was neat, lawns manicured and well maintained.

Gopi had passed by the temple road many times on his way to deliver mail. He had never found the time to enter the complex and instead always folded his hands in namaskar from the road. Appa, on the other hand, had a deep knowledge of temples, and studying their history was one of his hobbies.

He explained "There is an interesting legend behind this temple. Once in ancient times, there was an evil spirit a bhuta who was born when Lord Shiva fought with the Asura Andhaka. The bhuta performed severe penance and Shiva gave him a boon that allowed him to swallow the three worlds that make the cosmos. Accordingly, he began to stretch himself to occupy the heavens. This scared the gods who ensured that he fell to earth and did not achieve his aim. Once he fell, the gods used the opportunity to pin his body at five main points and immobilized him. The belief gave rise to the Vastupurusa or important parts of a plot of land where Vastu resides. The five Shiva lingams you see are the five points where the demon was pinned down. Lord Brahma could not undo the boon the Shiva gave. Hence, he ordained that the Vastu should remain where it was and that anyone who wanted to construct a structure had to appease the Vastu with food, fruit, and other offerings.

They entered the complex and stood in the inner courtyard. Appa turned towards Gopi

"Any questions? No? Okay. To continue, they say that an old temple was built during Vedic times at the spot where the Asura fell. The Chalukya Kings conquered this region in the 11th century and built this temple."

Gopi stood with his features distorted and suffused. Clearly, his mind was battling a complex issue.

Appa asked him "What is the matter?"

"I don't know. I can remember seeing this complex, the carvings, the statues, and the lingams. I get the feeling I have seen these things earlier, even come here before."

"Well, have you?"

Lata broke in "No Appa. He has never come here even though I have asked him many times. Perhaps, he has seen drawings on the temple in books."

As Gopi turned to look closer into the corner, he saw something standing there. It was the headless apparition, pointing at the structure. *What! This thing is following me around when I am with my family!*

Rage overcame him and he rushed at the apparition to catch it. He stumbled over a step and fell. The injury was minor but his anger and outrage at the specter for following his family inflamed him. Appa and other people carried him and sat him under a tree.

Lata stood forlornly clutching the baby *what was wrong with my husband?*

The old priest of the temple came over. Appa knew him and they went to a corner away from the two.

"Guruji, our postmaster Gopi is behaving very strangely since the past few days. He says that he saw the headless postman. Gopi is a good man. What is the problem?"

The old priest had spent many decades in the village and knew everybody there. He was also aware of the legend of the headless postman. He was in deep thought for a while Appa waited patiently.

Then he said "I fear Gopi is possessed by an evil spirit. This spirit has entered his body and is getting more and more powerful. Soon it will gain control of the mind and then Gopi will die."

"What can we do to help? I can't just stand and watch while this good man and his family are destroyed."

"The evil spirit has to be exorcised and driven away. We have to go to Saundatti where Goddess Yellamma resides. I know the chief Māṭagāti Vaidya, the main witchdoctor priest. We will see that can be done."

When the plans were announced, Gopi became belligerent and obstinately refused to get exorcised. His ego prevented him from accepting that he was possessed.

He asked "How will it look the next time I deliver mails? People will ask me about the evil spirit. Everyone respects me here and I will look foolish"

Lata cried, threw tantrums, and tore her hair; finally, he agreed. He was extremely skeptical of such practices, but he loved his wife and was ready to take this step for her.

Chapter 6
The Exorcism and the Unraveling of the Family Curse

Appa, Guruji, Gopi, and Lata went one afternoon to Saundatti and the temple of goddess Yellamma. Built in the 3 Century CE, the temple on the Saundatti Bettal has seen many additions and improvements. The temple is dedicated to Goddess Yellamma or Renuka, the goddess of fertility and Saptamatrika, the seven divine mothers. It was believed that anyone who worshipped at the temple would see their problems such as infertility and financial woes, family problems disappear. On the outskirts of the temple, there is a thriving practice of witchdoctors who took up exorcism to drive away evil spirits.

The group first prayed at the temple and as night fell, they descended the slope to the area where the exorcism practices were conducted. It was a small plot in a thickly wooded part of the forest and approached by a small footpath. The river Malaprabha River flowed majestically below.

The Māṭagāti Vaidya welcomed them and then looked at Gopi. He gave him a concoction of milk and bhang mixed with sugar. The drink had a soporific effect and rendered docile belligerent hosts such as Gopi and their infestations.

The ground was beaten hard to make it firm and then smeared with cow dung. Rice powder and chalk were used to create rangoli patterns and rectangular spaces on the floor. These spaces were drawn in concentric circles around the center, where a fire was burning.

The squares represented a set of demons, and while there were more than 87,000 demons, only a few spaces were made to represent the main ones of a group of demons. The subject of the ritual was seated in a circle. Flowers, banana leaves were liberally spread across the arena along with clay pots, whisk brooms, and some hens which sat in enclosures at the back. A hen would be sacrificed only if the ritual or a demon demanded.

There was another darker aspect that was not openly acknowledged. This was the human sacrifice for tantric magic, very powerful magic used for only the most severe infestations. Appa and Guruji did not consider the human sacrifice ritual.

Gopi was helped to his feet, the effects of Bhang still strong. He was in a trance but supported like a drunk by Appa and Guruji. He was seated in the circle facing east and flowers were arranged along the circumference. Drum beaters or dholak players and flute players, their faces and torsos smeared with ash were seated outside the circle. A small fire was started.

The master Māṭagāti vaidya shouted "Yajamana (gentleman), you are placed in the circle and as I start asking questions you have to answer. The drums will beat continually, rattling, and confusing the demon inside you. It will want to come out but it cannot escape the circle and we can trap it."

The master started his intonation of mantras and formulaic invocations to the great gods and Devi

Yelamma. Then he started singing with full force, all the while looking at Gopi closely. His objective was to find out the name of the demon so that the appropriate spell could be used. He blew hard at the smoke and brandished a broom. The rituals began.

Gopi slowly swayed to the beats of the drums and the sound of the flute, moving slowly where he sat. The drums would slow down, then pick up a pace to thunder, making him jerk and struggle

The master shouted, "Come on Yajamana, tell me your name."

"Gopinath Kulkarni."

"What are your caste and gotra?"

"Brahmin, Vasistha gotra."

"Where were you born?"

"Dharwad."

"What is your father's and grandfather's name?"

"Father's name is Vitthal Rama Kulrani, grandfathers name is Narayan Rao Kulkarni."

"What is your great-grandfather's name?"

Gopi started trembling and shaking. He tried to get up from the circle, but the master's assistants forced him down.

The master repeated the question "What is your great-grandfather's name?"

The master repeated the question a few more times and it only served to drive Gopi to anger. No answer was forthcoming. He thrashed about and would have run away but for the three stout, strong, and large assistants who struggled to hold him.

The master noted the answers with a frown. *When the question about his great-grandfather was asked, Gopi showed a strength that was almost equal to that of three wrestlers. His rage and perhaps fear gave him this strength and he wanted to break free.* The master moved back, wanting to allow Gopi to calm down. In this present state, any further questions would cause a nervous breakdown.

He signaled the musicians to continue their songs. He asked them to play a repertoire of old folk songs that were popular about 70 years back. The intention was to have the old spirit – if any – in Gopi's body to manifest itself when the favorite music was played. It was also possible that the spirit would try to harm Gopi in anger for being woken up.

The musicians moved between different ballads and songs by Bhagwan Basavanna, several vacahanas, and then one of them started playing a racy ballad Periyapattanada Kalaga. This song narrated the battle and tales of bravery between a King of Mysore and the King of Periyapattana.

Gopi stopped thrashing as the song started. Then he began to sing in an old Kannada dialect that was prevalent among the upper castes some decades back. The Master and the musicians noted with satisfaction that at least one doorway to see the demon had opened.

The drums started with a crescendo and then settled to a steady beat as the Master came close to Gopi.

"Why have you entered this body?"

"I have not entered this body."

"What do you want from Gopi? He will do what you want if you promise to leave his body."

"I have not entered this body."

"Who are you?"

"Someone ancient that Gopi knows."

"Why have you entered this body?"

"I am in his blood from the beginning."

And so it went, for quite some time. Nothing was happening. Matagati Vaidya eventually stopped the rituals since there was nothing to exorcise. Besides, Gopi would be hurt psychologically beyond recovery if this ritual continued.

The master offered another drink to Gopi to counter the sedative. His assistants carried Gopi to a hut beyond and Lata sat with him, sick with worry. Gopi laid his head on her lap and slept.

****

The master motioned Appa and Guruji aside.

"The yajamana is not possessed by any external spirit."

"What! Then what about the answers to your questions and dancing to the music?"

"I think it is a family curse. It appears that an ancestor, probably his great grandfather or another past forefather has not been appeased. Maybe, they did a bad deed, killed someone, and did not let the soul of the reclaimed person to be liberated? Do you know anything about his great grandfather? Yajamana goes violent when he is mentioned."

Appa replied "We do not know. Our employee records only ask for the father's name and place of birth."

The master said "As I said, it is possible that the great grand-father did something evil. His progeny wanted to remove all association with the person fearing that the stigma would haunt them. Over the generations, no trace of the person remains in the memory."

Guruji asked "Master, what about the headless apparition that haunts him?"

"Well, there was no sign of the apparition. It does not inhibit his body, else it would have identified itself. Yajamana must have heard or read stories of this ghost and decided to use its manifestation."

Appa asked, "What do we do now?"

"There is nothing we can do now. Let things remain as they are. Always keep someone with him when he goes out to deliver letters, and when he returns home. I feel that he will get over this spirit."

Chapter 7
The Dig

The exorcism had not cast out any evil spirit. However, Gopi was now a nervous and angry wreck. He huddled in his house angry and resentful at the manner in which people looked at him. Every sound the wind made played on his nerves. Each time the wind whistled through the roofing tiles, it sounded like the headless cyclist's breath. Night came, and with it fear for his family. The flickering kerosene lamp cast vivid mysterious patterns on the walls. With every gust of wind, the patterns seemed to be reaching out for him.

He yearned for one more encounter with the specter. He was prepared to send it to hell and back. What did it think? That he would become a gibbering victim to its terror tactics? One more encounter, just one more is all that he asked. He was not a victim. He would put an end to this nonsense. Enough was enough.

Sleep was farthest from Gopi's mind. Then he remembered the buried piece of sacking that he had seen from the window a few weeks back. The sack started eating into his mind, drawing him in, urging and goading him to get up and dig it up that very night.

Eager to investigate he took a pickaxe and the lamp and went out. The rain had stopped and the moon shone through tendrils of clouds. The piece of sacking lay where he had left it all those days ago, immersed in a small pool of water.

Gopi tugged at the sacking, and it started to come free in the wet soil. It seemed to be snagged by something underneath and he wanted to dig it free. Something swooped through the night sky and brushed his head making him jerk. It was an owl.

The bushes that made the hedge of his cottage rustled with the wind. The branches, heavy with rainwater, dipped and swung, showering him with each passing gust.

The first few hits with the pickaxe loosened the earth. He tugged at the sacking. Nothing happened. Something was holding it in the ground. Putting aside the pickaxe, he caught hold of the sack and pulled with both hands. The sacking tore loose, with the bottom still buried in the ground. Something dull glittered in the moonlight, and he bent down, tugging at the piece still stuck in the ground.

The sack came loose still held by something under the ground. Then Gopi saw the number on the sack '971'. *The torn page in the registry, employee number 971 – Gopal Rao – his beheading – his hasty burial ... Was this the spot where the wretched soul lay buried?'*

Eager to explore, he dug further and found that the sack was snagged on a rectangular piece of wood with a sign carved on the face. Carefully he dug with his fingers and brought out the wooden piece.

It had carvings and names of gods in Sanskrit. Figures of gods were carved on the face. *He had seen these motifs recently. Where?... Yes, it was at the temple; these carvings were from the temple. But how did the carvings appear on this piece and what was it doing here?* He had no answers.

The moon went behind the clouds and it started raining again. The hedge bushes parted, a shadow fell on him, and he found himself looking up into the maws of the headless rider. The rain fell directly into the hollow of the collar, where the head should have been, and bloodied water spurted forth in small droplets.

The apparition lifted its arms, beckoning him to follow, urging him to come forward. Gopi shook in anger at this apparition since it had ruined his routine and it had dared to come near his family. He wanted to grab and shake it but felt strangely powerless and weak-willed. It appeared to have cast some sort of hypnotic spell on him and he was unable to resist despite wanting to.

In a trance, he followed the specter, unwilling yet unresisting, as it turned and glided through the forest. It seemed to go on forever, and Gopi followed. Then it finally stopped at the very edge of the cliff overlooking a lake created by the dam backwaters. The rains had stopped and the moon glowed, illuminating the countryside in soft light. The apparition seemed to point at a small island in the middle of the lake.

The apparition dove into the water and started swimming towards the island, looking back to urge him to follow. The sheer exertion of the evening and the stress took its toll and Gopi fell on the precipice in a swoon, the sack and wooden board clutched in his hand.

When he felt himself jerk awake, the rain had stopped and the sun had risen beyond the treetops. A search party, led by Appa and Lata found him on the cliff, and they carried him back. It was late in the morning when the chattering birds woke him. He lay on the bed, with the wood piece and the sack on the floor.

****

The night's events were vivid in his mind. *It seemed that the spirit did not wish to kill him. It could have easily done so if it wished. Instead, it had wanted Gopi to go to the island. Why, and why him?* He would not rest until he found the answer.

Gopi examined the piece of wood carefully and realized that it had once been part of a motif on a door. A series of flower patterns, and symbols of gods, were engraved along the length. The figure of Yellamma, the local goddess, was engraved in the middle. The corner had broken off.

Two small holes on the sides of the panel with streaks of rust showed that nails had been used to fasten the piece to the door. Small scratch marks ran across the face of the piece. They could have been caused by a small animal, or by raking fingernails as someone struggled in his death throes. He was driven by an urgent need to know details of the panel. Who best to ask but the village carpenter? He deiced to meet the carpenter at the earliest.

Get a grip on yourself Gopi, he muttered to himself. *It was time to resume his work. Too many days of absenteeism and he would be sure to lose his job.* He finished his bath, performed pooja, and took off for work.

He reached the post office to meet the silent, questioning eyes of his colleagues. None wanted to ask him directly but everyone wanted to know about his wanderings. Curious villagers turned up and found some pretext to look and talk with him, and after seeing him, they sadly shook their heads and told each other that the fellow was a goner.

The morning passed in a whirl of activity. By afternoon, his work was over, and he set out to meet the village carpenter. He saw him sitting in front of his hut, sawing away at a plank. On seeing Gopi, he got up and folding his hands in greeting, and asked him to come inside.

Postmen and the school teacher were the only literate people in the area, and they were well respected. The carpenter had also heard about Gopi's encounter with the headless ghost, and he was curious to know about it.

After exchanging pleasantries, Gopi showed the piece of wood to the carpenter asking him where it came from. It had a fine scent and the carpenter looked closely at it.

"Sandalwood. This must a part of the panel of a pooja room. The design is rather old fashioned. I have never seen such a pattern other than in old temples, where did saheb find this?'

Not wanting to give the details to the carpenter, Gopi made up some story of finding it washed up in the stream.

The carpenter raised his arms helplessly, perhaps his grandfather would know.

"Is he here? Can we ask him?"

The grandfather was very old and was sleeping in a corner. He was almost gone and just holding on to life.

Softly nudging him awake and saying that the old man was deaf, the carpenter asked him.

"Ajja, look. The postmaster sahib has come to meet you and ask a few questions. Please look here."

He showed the wooden piece to Ajja. The old man squinted, brought it close to his eyes, felt it with his gnarled fingers, and started to cry. He replies were incoherent, and Gopi had to strain to catch what was said.

"Alas, Hire (elder) Dhanyaru, such a fine family, so kind-hearted. Then the eldest son took over the estate and all started going down."

The old man lapsed into meaningless jabber then became coherent.

"Yes, he had prepared the pooja room….Dhanyaru wanted it to look like the Panchalingeshwara temple. …. very nicely decorated ….fancy carvings … all made of sandalwood and teak … he had this headpiece carved … it was placed on top of the idol of Lord Shiva … such an inauspicious event … the cut-off head … blood spilled……..'

The old man dozed off to sleep, tears rolling from his eyes. The carpenter led Gopi out, nothing more could be known.

****

Gopi wanted to know the location of the old house where Desai, the landlord once lived and where the postmen had allegedly been beheaded. Perhaps the actual site would disclose something. He took Appa along to the land registrar's office.

The Registrar said "Dam waters now flow over the vast acres that the Landlord owned. The whole area is underwater. Any secret the place held is lost forever."

This was not true. He had seen the temple the other night.

Gopi said "Sahib, I had gone the other night to the top of the precipice that looks over the dam backwaters. I did see the island and the temple. It is there."

The Registrar replied "Post Master Sahib that is not possible. The estate of the landlord is the deepest water. It is always covered with water. Yes, there was a small hillock on which the house and temple once stood, but the dam swallowed it up. You must have imagined it."

Confused, Gopi wondered about the island, and the trees he had seen. *Had he imagined them? Was he imagining the apparition? None had seen it except him. Well, maybe...*

Gopi and Appa left for the post office and Appa offered to drop him home. The tree-lined path stood in front of him, and he dreaded going through it again. There was a longer circuitous track over a hill that bypassed the path and they decided to take it.

Small bushes and rocks littered the track as they climbed the hill. A small temple with an idol of the village deity, goddess Yellamma stood at the top. Gopi stopped to rest and after bowing to the Devi, turned to look at the magnificent scenery down below.

The dam backwaters flowed below, touching the foothills. Far away, he could see the dam sluice gates. The valley through which the river flowed had lush green forests, swaying in the wind. To the left, he could see his village and could guess the approximate position of his house. To the right were green forests that extended to meet the horizon, covered under an intermittent mist.

With a start, he realized that the landlord's farms and house would have been on the slope on the far right. Through the rolling mists, he could make out a hillock that formed an island and a small structure in the distance. Part of a wall was dimly visible. The wall, broken in places, ran south and ended in a canopy that would have been the main house.

Was this the Landlord's house? Perhaps the dam waters had spared the cursed house, not willing to sully itself with the unholy structure. Did the solution to his torment lie there? He had to find out.

Going down the hill was much easier, and soon, he was inside his home. The next two days were holidays, and he decided to explore the structure he had seen from the hilltop. Appa had dropped by.

He casually mentioned, "Look, Sahib; you can apply for an immediate transfer to another far off location. There, you will not see these things, and you will be at peace."

Gopi got up. "Transfer? Why? What will people think of me? That I am a coward and ran away when I could not handle something?"

Appa calmed him down. "I was only thinking of you and your family. That's all."

"Never mind my health Appa. I will be fine once this thing is over. Anyway, Appa. That hillock, island, and the broken walls, did they belong to the landlord?"

Appa stared at him in wonder and puzzlement.

"What hillock? What island and wall? There was only water."

"Oh no, Appa. I'm talking about the island we saw from the hill."

"Sahib, you are again imagining things. There is nothing there but hills and water. The land registrar told you that all the structures and land are now under deep water. There is nothing but hills and forests on the banks. The dam had swallowed the old village and the Landlord's house. How could you have seen it?"

Snorting in frustration and anger, Gopi went inside. Everyone was lying, they were being over-protective. He knew what he saw. He had seen the house and its outer walls. Well, there was only one way to find out – he had no choice but to go there. For his sanity and the safety of his wife and baby, he had to solve the mystery.

Chapter 8
Journey to the Island

Early the next morning, before his wife woke up, he went down to the lakeshore, met a fisherman, and asked him to take him across.

The fisherman was not willing to do this "No Saheb! The other side is taboo. There are whirlpools and anyone who went there never came back."

Gopi offered him five rupees. He would hire the boat for a day. After many threats and counter-arguments, the fisherman finally relented and handed over the boat. Gopi tried out the boat and kept his sack with the broken wooden panel and the torn sacking he had dug up.

"Turn back by afternoon Sahib as the current starts flowing back to the far side. You will remain stranded on the far shore if you delay. Watch out for rocks and whirlpools. There is a water skin with fresh water, some food, a kerosene lamp, some bandages, matches, and an ax if you need them."

****

While Gopi was not an expert at handling boats, he had ridden in them often and could manage the vessel. He set off, rowing with slow leisurely strokes in the direction where he had seen the structure. He had plotted an approximate course that would take him to the required location.

The small waves had turned choppy and the undertow was deciding his course. Gopi hunched forward and started rowing forcefully. The normally placid waters seemed to have strong undercurrents, and they pulled him across to the far side.

After half an hour of rowing, a small rock loomed in the early morning mist. It rose from the lake depths and stood like a sentinel guarding the temple. He pulled around it and then an undercurrent caught him. The current carried him steadily forward with force, and all he had to do was to slip an oar on each side and paddle in the right direction.

The hillock and the ruined walls appeared as faint silhouettes. They became sharper as the boat approached the structure. Gopi gauged the distance to the edifice and paddled to the right. The current was taking him along where he wanted to go.

He saw a piece of driftwood, floating along and then suddenly it whipped forward going incredibly fast. He watched with rapt attention as it bounced among the waves, then circled around very fast before it disappeared into the water.

Whirlpool!

With wide eyes, he saw the whirlpool just ahead and to his left. The rim of the whirlpool went round in crazy circles, now rising and then falling, white froth dripping from the edges. It hissed and bubbled like a serpent as it went around moving with the current, sucking whatever came its way.

Gopi pulled at the oars in the opposite direction with all he had, trying to get away. The outer edge of the cone of the whirlpool was just a few oar lengths from his boat, and Gopi got a close look at the terrifying sight inside.

The cone went around in a hypnotic swirl, the walls seemed incredibly smooth and edged with a white forth that broke every now and then to send up a fine spray. The mouth opened and closed, giving out large bubbles. Gopi fought hard, feeling the boat slip into the funnel, one end hung in the mouth and as the boat spun fast, he felt his head going giddy.

The next instant, he was out of the grip, as the whirlpool threw his boat away. The hillock was nearby and he limply pulled the boat ashore. Then he sank to the ground trembling and weak with exhaustion.

****

A while later, Gopi staggered up and marked his bearings. The structure he had seen would be to his right. The path was thick with bushes and water ran through the underbrush. Drawing out the ax he had taken from the boat, he hacked his way through the dense underbrush and entered a small clearing.

He could make out a masonry construction under patches of slippery green moss. *Strange, the jungle has grown all over but this small patch has no trees or bushes. Was this place so evil that even the jungle refused to claim it?*

The moss clung to the walls dripping and wet. He scraped it and saw the huge outer wall underneath. It had been built a long time back as a mini fortress, and the wall was about five feet thick. As per ancient vastushastra, the main door would be facing northeast and the pooja room would be on the same side.

Stepping carefully, he made his way across the wall and then saw a raised portion, where the wall met the main doorway. A narrow passage ran along the inner length, and Gopi guessed this must be where the soldiers stood on guard.

He approached the raised portion and peered over the side to see a large doorframe. Climbing down carefully, he stood in front of the huge stone doorway. The wooden doors had rotted long ago and only rusting hinges remained.

Then he saw the goddess Yellamma's image, carved on the wooden frame that still remained with a part broken off. From his satchel, he pulled out the wooden piece that he had dug out from his garden and fit it on the door. It was a perfect fit.

The wind had started blowing with full force, and in the distance, he could hear jackals howling. The wind seemed to be whispering something. Gopi listened intently, *Come, step inside* it seemed to be hiss.

That was when he realized he had company. Turning back quickly, he thought he saw something streak into the bushes. The jungle sounds had almost stopped, and he could hear his own breath, coming in harsh rasps.

He stepped through the doorway carefully and was inside. The roof had fallen in many places and he could make out piles of rubble everywhere.

He made his way to the courtyard where the cows would have been tethered. Just beyond was the raised platform, running along the length of the house and which would lead to the rooms where people lived. To the left, he could see a small platform on which the Landlord probably reclined and governed.

A small noise behind made him turn.

There! Something streaked again across in the background.

He shouted "Who is there? Come out and show yourself. I know you are there."

His voice resounded through the structure. Nothing moved and he could hear his voice echoing through the ruins.

He saw a couple of steps to the right and these led to a room with a low ceiling and a deep pit. *This would be the granary, where food grains were stored.* He turned back the way he had come and saw another small passage.

The passage led to a small room, and Gopi realized that he was in front of the sanctum of the pooja room. A stone statue of the village deity stood guard at the entrance. Arranged in the room were the five Shiva lingams he had seen in the temple back in the village.

A rusted hook swung above from the ceiling, and this was where the temple bell would have hung. Normally visitors rang the bell before entering the sanctum and prayed at the Shiva Lingams. This bell was long gone and the chain holding the bell to the hook was rusted.

The landlord had been a devotee of Shiva and he had taken care to replicate the interior of the Panchalingeshwara temple and the Garbhagruhas in his home. While the ancient temple had figures carved in granite, the skills needed for granite sculpture was not available locally. Besides, granite carvings would take decades to complete. Hence, he had asked carpenters to carve out the motifs in sandalwood.

The walls and the ceiling were still covered with sandalwood. Long immersion in water had made the wood moist and soft, and some pieces had fallen off while others hung limp.

A cold apprehension filled him as he approached the room. *Was this the end of his troubles? Was this the place where he would find answers to his torment?*

****

He slowly stepped inside the lowered doorway and stood in the sanctum sanctorum. It was dark and he had to peer to see what was inside. Some parts of the inner walls were covered with marble the slabs broken and dirt spilling out while the other areas had sandalwood. In the corner was a pedestal where the Shiva idol would have been placed. At the base of the pedestal were small furrows to allow the water used in the pooja to run off to a small cistern and to the garden beyond. The five Shiva lingams were arranged so that water from the idol would wash the lingams.

Small furrows were carved in the granite pedestal. The furrows were encrusted with grime and dirt. They had carried the holy water for a long time and now stood neglected and broken. The walls had small niches for oil lamps. Patches of dark oil were still visible. In the corner, just behind the pedestal was a small mound.

Something moved on the floor, glistening and wet. Something was flowing from the mound and running through the furrows, drenching his foot. He looked down uncomprehending. Then the realization flooded him. It was blood. *Blood oozing out of the walls, and lamps, and running in small threads along the floor.*

He turned back in panic and froze. His heart almost stopped and then speeded up like never before. The apparition stood at the door. The headless apparition had finally come seeking him. It stood silently, a bleeding head held in its hands. It spoke to his mind telepathically and he could understand what it was saying.

"Dhanyaru."

As it came nearer, images flashed in his head. With deep loathing, he realized this was his family's horrid past.

He was the inheritor, the descendent of the evil landlord.

His brain numbed with the onslaught of images from the past.

The landlord was performing pooja. Just then, the postman entered, eager to receive some baksheesh when he delivered the letter and read it out... the postman started reading. At first with confidence...then with a trembling voice as he read out the notice written by the district collector to confiscate the lands...

Respected Desai, Landlord. The government is constructing a dam in the area. To complete the construction, we are acquiring your land. Suitable compensation will be given to you as per the rules. We request you to vacate the holdings with immediate effect. Signed. Collector of Land, Hooli Tehsil.

The landlord got up then...cursing the collector...cursing the postman...he grabbed a sword in a scabbard hanging on the wall ...unsheathed it and swung at the postman, slashing his chest... the postman stumbled back...went crashing down against the idol and tried weakly to scramble out the door ...As he visibly weakened in sheer desperation he clung to the sandalwood carving at the door, breaking a fragment as he collapsed...the landlord swung his sword again and cut off the postman's head.

--the head...the head...that was what it wanted.

Now, where did he bury the head.. there! Under the mound.

Gopi dug the dirt frantically, his fingers bleeding from the rough soil and gravel, but continued nevertheless.

The apparition, now hovered behind his back, the skeletal hands gripping a sword as it prepared to cut off Gopi's head.

Just then, Gopi's fingers touched something smooth. He brushed the soil off it and it seemed to glisten in the light. Hurriedly, he pulled out the skull completely and offered it to the apparition.

The sword clattered to the ground as the apparition bowed before Gopi Desai Dhanyaru, the great-grandson of the landlord.

A deep sigh seemed to emanate from the walls as the ghost accepted the skull, and fitted it back onto its neck. Then it retreated, going through the walls, and walking away. *That is all it ever wanted. This saga is now ended.*

A deep sound startled Gopi. The walls started to crumble, and the floor began to tremble.

Water began to seep in from the walls, and soon it would inundate the structure. He rushed out, stumbled through the creepers. At the shore, he saw the boat bobbing as waves lapped.

He jumped into the boat and started rowing, the ebb tide carrying him away. There were a huge thunderclap and a rush of air, which propelled his boat forward. He looked back and saw the island disappear under the waters of the dam. A dust cloud appeared over the waters and slowly started following Gopi.

Gopi knew that he had to go fast. He pulled out and rowed like one possessed, trying to escape from the island and his past. He was just a hundred meters away from the now sunk island when the whirlpool appeared.

It glided across the waters in a whorl of hissing, gurgling, and bubbles and rushed to intercept the boat. The wind and waves changed direction, pushing the boat forward towards the whirl of death.

It was clear that the island wanted to take the descendant of the landlord. There was no escaping the hiss of water as it gripped his boat and started spinning it around the periphery and pulling the boat into the funnel.

Slowly at first, then rapidly, Gopi felt the pressure of the spin almost tearing his body. As he sank into the funnel, he looked up. The apparition watched him, the skull in its place and the skeleton full.

As he started sinking deeper into the funnel, the last image in Gopi's mind was of Lata and the baby.

****

The old man came out of his trance and whispered "Search parties went around the shore searching for Gopi. The fisherman had told the search parties that he had lent Gopi a boat and that the postmaster had been speaking of an island far beyond before he left with the boat. They found the battered boat, but there was no sign of Gopi. Lata and baby left the village shortly, and no one knew what happened to them. After Gopi's disappearance, the ghost also vanished."

****

The old man dozed off to sleep, tired after his story.

I thanked the old man for the story. *Fascinating story. Maybe I could use it. It would a good piece in a horror anthology collection.*

As I got up to leave, I glanced at the satchel on the bench. The hair on my scalp stiffened, my flesh crawled with goose pimples. The satchel's brass plate twinkled as I stared at the number on it - 971.

--END--

About the Author

Shashi Kadapa lives in Pune, India. He is the managing editor of ActiveMuse, a journal of literature. His short stories have appeared in anthologies of Casagrande Press, Alien Dimensions #11, Carpathia Publishing, Spadina Literary Review, The Times of India, and Debonair.

His most recent stories are forthcoming in anthologies of Agorist Writers, Escaped Ink, and Witching Hour. Shashi is also currently working on a book of short stories and a novel.

Website: http://www.activemuse.org
Twitter: https://twitter.com/active_muse
Facebook: https://www.facebook.com/shashi.kadapa
Email: shashikadapa@gmail.com

CPSIA information can be obtained
at www.ICGtesting.com
Printed in the USA
BVHW031725161120
593415BV00005B/484